MARKED FOR RISK

SUSAN HAYES

Marked For Risk (Book five of the Crashed and Claimed series)

First print Publication: April 2023

Editor: Amanda Brown

Cover Art: Croco Designs

Published by: Black Scroll Publications Ltd

*For my parents, I wouldn't be here without your love
and constant support as I chase after my dreams.
This story is also dedicated to a wonderful crew of
gamers who make me laugh every time I see them
online. Long live the Black Bulls!*

ABOUT THE BOOK

She thought Cupid's arrow would never find her... love sent a missile instead.

Being the onboard matchmaker for an interstellar dating cruise isn't the most exciting job in the world, but that's fine. Joy likes things to be calm and orderly. Then the ship gets attacked, and her captain orders her into an escape pod with two VIPs and instructions to keep everyone alive.

Crashing on an unknown planet is one excursion she never planned for. The wildlife is dangerous, the terrain is treacherous, and the only help available comes in the form of a tall, horned alien with the sex appeal of a rockstar and a stubborn streak wider than the Milky Way.

He's certain she belongs to *him*. She's convinced he's crazy. She's got a long list of reasons why it could never work, but the big, sexy alien has his charms... and he's willing to use them all to get what he wants. *Her.*

After years of helping others look for love, this might be Joy's chance to find it for herself... but only if she's willing to take the risk.

**Buckle up. This sci-fi romance contains an alien with fur, fangs, horns, and a very possessive attitude when it comes to the woman he's claimed for his own.*

1

After nearly ten years at the same job, Joy had moments when she thought she'd seen it all. The universe invariably took that as a challenge and threw something even stranger her way, but this time the universe had outdone itself.

The entire cruise had been one what-the-hells moment after another. Several of the guests had gotten into a brawl while vying for the attentions of one particularly wealthy male looking for a match. The attention-grabbing and undignified display had resulted in the male raska-shi choosing to contract with all three women, though they didn't discover that fact until after the mating contracts were signed.

That was why she encouraged their guests to carefully consider any offer before signing. She even gave a seminar on mating contracts and volunteered to act as an advisor, but rarely did anyone take her up on the offer. These women all wanted to escape their current lives and had convinced themselves that anything else was an improvement.

These days, most of them were simply trading one set of hardships for another. It hadn't always been this way. When Joy had first joined Captain Perez and the crew of the *Bountiful Harvest,* their galactic matchmaking cruises had been exactly that—a chance for unattached males of various species to meet and mingle with human women. Sparks flew, romances blossomed, and while not every match was perfect, each cruise produced multiple success stories. As the ship's event coordinator and matchmaker, Joy took pride in every match she helped to make.

As the years passed, though, things changed. Instead of life-mates, the males attending the events wanted breeders or concubines. Mating contracts that protected all the parties had morphed into cold-hearted business arrangements. Some bordered on conditions that resembled slavery more than anything remotely romantic.

"Captain, I think our event coordinator is broken," First Officer Mika Hooper's comment pulled Joy out of her dark thoughts and back to the present.

"What? Why?" She raised her head and looked over to the first officer's workstation. It wasn't necessary since Joy saw her environment through sensors and not with her eyes, but people reacted better if she made an effort to face their direction when conversing.

"I've never seen you make that face before." Mika had scrunched her face up like she'd bitten into something sour. "In fact, I think this is the first time I've seen you without a smile. You usually have one plastered onto your face no matter what's happening. I actually thought your face was frozen that way, you know, after the accident."

Joy didn't react to Mika's goading. The woman took a perverse sort of pleasure in needling people, and Joy had learned to stay quiet and let the captain deal with it.

"Hooper." Captain Jodi Perez's tone was as cold as the void outside. "I'm not going to tell you again. You want to be a jerk, do it inside your own head. The rest of us don't need to hear it."

"What?" Hooper shrugged in a half-hearted attempt to look innocent. "She's a smiler. That's all I was saying."

Joy returned to work. Space on the *Harvest* was limited, so she didn't have an office. Instead, she used one of auxiliary workstations on the bridge, even though she wasn't designated bridge crew. The close proximity also made it easy to keep the captain up to date with event scheduling and any problems that cropped up among their guests.

It was her job to keep the guests entertained and happy for the whole cruise, whether they were docked or in transit. At the beginning of each trip that was easy enough. All the passengers were hopeful and full of enthusiasm. They were in the final leg of the journey now, though, which meant the handful of guests still on board were dealing with rejection and self-doubt.

She understood exactly what they were going through. There'd been a time she'd had so many hopes and dreams for her own life... but that was long ago. Before the accident that took her sight and left her scarred and broken.

That's why she poured her heart and soul into finding matches for the women who signed up for these matchmaking cruises. She wanted them to find the love and happiness she'd never have.

"Bashir. Do you have a few minutes?" Captain Perez asked.

"Of course, Captain. Out here or in your ready room?"

Jodi cocked her head to the side and then laughed. "You're hoping for a coffee made from my personal stash. Aren't you?"

"Yes, I am," Joy admitted without a trace of guilt. Everyone on board knew the captain's coffee was the best. No one had any idea where she got it from or what magical process made it so damned good.

"You caught me in a generous mood. Hooper, you have the bridge."

"Yes, ma'am," Hooper acknowledged.

Joy followed the captain off the bridge and into her office. It was barely bigger than a closet, but it provided the most valuable commodity on the ship—a chance to converse in private.

The moment the door closed, Jodi pointed back toward the bridge. "I wanted you to hear it first. That was Hooper's final mistake. I intend to fire her the moment this trip is over."

Joy nodded and exhaled in relief. "Thank you. She's been... challenging to work with."

Jodi snorted. "You mean she's a bitch and a bully."

"I did, but in my line of work, it pays to be diplomatic at all times." If she filtered everything she said, it became easier to avoid slipping up and saying something harsh to a paying guest.

"I'd last about thirty seconds if I had to do your job." Jodi sat down behind her small desk and gestured for Joy to do the same. "Speaking of which, anything I need to know? How are the remaining guests coping?"

"The usual issues. I'm concerned that some of them are desperate enough to be vulnerable to the predators who will be waiting to pounce at our next stop."

"Have you told Maddison about that issue, yet?" Jodi asked while tapping a request for two coffees into the dispenser behind her.

Maddison Summers was the new owner of the *Harvest*. She'd come on board at their last stop and would travel with them for a time to get to know the ship and her crew. No one knew much about her other than the fact she'd gotten ownership of the ship and the matchmaking cruise business as part of her divorce settlement with the previous owner.

"Not yet. I have a meeting scheduled with her this afternoon, and I'll explain the problem then. That way she can see it for herself when we reach our next destination."

Jodi grimaced. "I can't stand watching it happen and knowing we can do nothing to stop it."

"Me either. Hopefully Maddison will hate it just as much, and we can convince her to make some changes."

The conversation paused while the captain turned to retrieve two steaming mugs of coffee from the dispenser. She pushed one across the desk to Joy... and then all hell broke loose.

The deck beneath her bucked and shuddered hard

enough her cup of coffee spilled and rolled off the table.

Jodi jumped to her feet with her cup still in her hand. "Shit! Back to your station."

They rushed back onto the bridge.

"Report! And someone mute those alarms already." The captain's voice was almost drowned out by a deep, metallic groan followed by several creaks that sounded like they came from the hull.

Joy had never heard anything like it, but she knew it wasn't a good sound. She hurried back to her station and strapped in. She'd gone over emergency procedures with the passengers so many times they should know what to do, but experience had taught her that at least some of them would panic. *You can't do anything about that right now*, she reminded herself. The captain had ordered her to her station, so that's where she'd stay.

"Hyperdrive engine two is offline, Captain. We've fallen back into normal space," Hooper reported.

"Dammit! Get me engineering. They promised me their repairs would hold until we made port," Jodi barked and then turned toward the ship's helmsman. Where are we right now? Whose territory are we in?"

Because she wasn't bridge crew, Joy had nothing to do but listen. What she heard next made the hairs on the back of her neck rise as a chill chased down her spine.

"We're in... shit. I don't understand how this happened, ma'am." The helm officer stared at her monitor in obvious confusion. "According to the nav system, we're in verexi space."

That shouldn't be possible. The verexi weren't classified as a hostile race, but they were fiercely territorial, xenophobic, and a generally unpleasant species. They also considered humans to be lesser beings and refused to have anything to do with them. If they learned the *Harvest* was in their territory, they'd be more likely to attack than to offer assistance. She just had to hope they got out of here before that happened.

Judging by the captain's stormy expression, her conversation with engineering wasn't going well, though so many technical terms were flying around Joy couldn't understand the details. Not that she needed to. Her job was to manage the guests, not the ship.

"Captain, we've got incoming fire," Hooper almost shouted, her voice cracking slightly.

"Son of a bitch. Brace!" Jodi ordered. "Who fired? From where?"

More alarms sounded. The captain looked grim as she activated the ship-wide comms and called all off-duty personnel to the bridge.

The bridge door slid open a few seconds later, allowing Maddison Summers with her personal assistant—and sometimes bodyguard—Loris, to join them.

"What's happening?" Maddison asked. Her complexion was ashen and she had the look of someone fighting back panic.

Jodi didn't answer. Instead, she pointed to an empty chair. "Sit down, strap in, and shut up. I'll explain if we live through the next few minutes."

To her credit, Maddison didn't protest. She just did as she was told.

The deck bucked again, and this time the lights flickered and died. The emergency lighting kicked in almost immediately, bathing the bridge in a reddish glow that did nothing to improve their situation.

Joy activated a feature of her coronet she rarely used while on the bridge and zoomed in to see what was showing on the captain's display. Damage reports filled the screen. It only took a brief look to know the *Harvest* was in trouble. Now she understood why none of the off-duty staff had made it to the bridge. Multiple hull breeches had exposed parts of the ship to vacuum, making it almost impossible to reach their area. Maddison and Loris had only made it because the captain had given them her cabin, which was right next to the bridge.

Were her friends and coworkers alright? What about the passengers? No doubt they'd be losing their minds by now. "How many escape pods deployed?" Jodi asked.

"Six deployed. But those bastards have shot down three of them." Hooper slammed her hands down on her console. We're sitting ducks out here! We're going to die."

"Keep it together, Hooper. We're not dead yet."

"Ma'am, we have another problem," the pilot called out over the din. "We're falling into the gravity well of a planet, and we only have partial power to our normal engines."

"Fuck!" Jodi swore, her composure cracking for a second. Then the captain schooled her features and got back to work.

"Joy, get me everything you can about that planet. Atmosphere, survivability. Can we breathe the air if we go down?"

"Yes, ma'am." Joy called up the data and sent the pertinent information to the captain's monitor. Everything she saw looked promising. The planet was uninhabited but had everything they'd need to survive until rescue.

The hull groaned, and the deck twisted and rippled as they dropped deeper into the planet's gravity well.

The captain bowed her head in defeat as she opened the ship-wide comms again. "This is the captain. I'm ordering everyone to abandon ship. I repeat. Abandon ship."

She turned toward Maddison and Loris. "That includes the two of you."

"I should stay," Maddison argued.

"No, ma'am. You need to board the command shuttle. Once we're inside the atmosphere, the autopilot can handle the descent and landing on its own."

"Where do we go?" Loris asked.

"That hatch over there," Jodi pointed and then spun to face Joy. "Bashir, you go with them and see to their safety. I'm counting on you."

Joy nodded and unclipped her harness.

"What the hell, Captain? You're sending the blind party planner? What the hell can she do to protect the VIPs?" Hooper rose from her chair, her face flushed and eyes wild. "I'll do it."

"Hooper! You will sit your ass down right now. Your place is here, ensuring we do everything possible to bring this ship down intact."

Joy moved quietly, trying to join Maddison and Loris and escort them to the access hatch without Hooper noticing.

It didn't work.

The first officer uttered a deranged howl and hurled herself at Joy. One second she was on her feet, and the next she was flying through the air, and the floor was rising up to meet her. Then everything went black.

2

Risk and his companions moved through the trees in their usual formation—with him taking point and the other two some distance behind. Vengeance and Havoc continued the same argument they'd been having since they'd met with Menace and his newly claimed female. They all had different ideas about how to approach any females they might encounter.

They had already learned that a ship with human females aboard had ejected several escape pods before crashing some distance away from their homes. Three of their brothers had found the pods and claimed the females.

Word spread quickly, and the rest of their clan had rushed to the crash site in hopes of finding other females. Unfortunately, the three of them were out hunting when the news came, so they'd been left behind. Not that he blamed his brothers for that. He'd have done the same thing in their place.

Vengeance didn't feel the same way. He envied Mayhem and Strife's good fortune. His anger only grew when they'd come across Menace and Hope while taking a shortcut that should lessen the distance between them and the other fa'rel. He wanted to charge ahead and deal with any problems later. As usual.

"Remember what the female said," Havoc growled at Vengeance. "We need to be gentle with these humans."

"If any are left by the time we reach them," Vengeance snarled. "We're moving too slowly."

Risk turned and bared his fangs at his brother. "Would you like to lead for a while, Venge? You can set whatever pace you like. If you're away from Havoc, maybe the two of you will stop arguing."

"I'm not arguing," Vengeance grumbled.

Risk slowed from a jog to a walk and then stopped completely so he could stare down his brothers. "You're *both* arguing. One of you wants to rush in. The other wants to make elaborate plans and consider every possible scenario. You're wrong."

The other two stopped in their tracks, clearly surprised by his outburst. He didn't lose his temper as often as the others, not even when they'd been in each other's company for more than a few hours. That was the real reason his companions were arguing. Between the time they'd spent hunting together and this new adventure, it was a wonder his brothers hadn't come to blows yet.

"We can't both be wrong," Vengeance said.

"Yeah, you can." He thumped a fist to his bare chest. "*My* plan is the right one."

"And what's your plan?" Havoc asked.

"Nice of you to finally ask," Risk said. In all the hours Venge and Havoc had argued, neither of them had bothered to ask his opinion. They'd assumed he'd side with one of them. In fact, they probably both thought he was on *their* side. He wasn't.

Both of them lapsed into silence and lowered their gaze for a moment, which Risk interpreted as something akin to an apology. Or at least as close to one as he would ever get. The fa'rel didn't do apologies. They'd fight and then forget about it. If things went too far, a gift might be offered, but that was all.

"We have no idea how any of this mating crap works. We've never *seen* a female before today. Assuming there are any survivors, don't you think we should get to know them before we decide we want to spend forever with one?" He pointed at Vengeance. "You want to charge in and claim one, but what if she doesn't like you? What if you don't like her?" As far as

Risk was concerned, spending the rest of his life bonded to someone he didn't like was a far worse fate than never having a mate at all.

Vengeance grimaced. "You think that could happen?"

Havoc scrubbed a hand through his beard and scowled. "When did you become the logical one?"

"Right after the two of you saw Menace's female and lost your fucking minds."

"But she was so beautiful," Havoc said, repeating the same thing he'd said when he'd met Hope.

Vengeance rolled his eyes and shoved Havoc with enough force to make the other male stagger. "Hope is pretty. My mate will be *beautiful*," he declared. "I will claim the best of them for myself."

Risk snarled at his brother. "That's not what Hope said. She told us to be gentle with the females. Remember?"

"No." Vengeance shook his head. "I don't remember that part."

"She said to be gentle, like Menace was with her." Havoc looked bemused. "I don't think that word translated correctly. Our brother is far from gentle."

All three of them chuckled and nodded in agreement, but Risk wasn't done talking. "Hope also said that if we were lucky, one of the females might choose to bond with us. *Might*," he stressed the word again. "We shouldn't assume we can simply lay claim to one of the females."

Vengeance growled. "I like my plan better."

This time, Havoc shoved Vengeance. "You would. Simple minds like simple plans. Risk is saying I'm right. We need a plan."

"That's not what I said!" Risk was ready to leave his brothers and make the rest of the journey alone. Havoc and Vengeance were his closest friends, but at times he wanted to grab them by their horns and shake them.

Havoc snarled and raised one hand, his claws extended.

Risk ignored the warning and stood his ground. The two of them stared at each other until Vengeance broke the tension by unslinging his pack and rummaging for a snack. "If we're going to stand around here for a while, I'm eating. You two do whatever it is you're doing."

Risk chuckled and Havoc relaxed enough to smile and say, "Food sounds good. We'll eat while Risk explains why we don't need a plan."

He ignored the jibe and searched his own pack for something to eat. Then, he leaned against a tree and explained.

"We need to aim for the middle ground somewhere between having no plan at all and having one that's too complex. There are too many unknowns."

Neither of his brothers looked convinced, but Risk was done with this conversation. He'd said his piece. Either the others listened, or they didn't. All of them were free to live any way they wished so long as their choices didn't harm the rest of the clan. They had fought and almost died gaining their freedom from the verexi. After a lifetime of imprisonment, torture, and experiments, every member of the clan valued their right to make their own choices above all else. They'd die before they let anyone take that from them again.

The three of them set out again after a brief rest and a snack. They ran through trees, leaping over fallen logs, moss-covered boulders, and anything else that blocked their way. Risk led, but the others were only a few steps behind. Before long they were racing each other through the forest, their disagreements forgotten.

They wouldn't stop until nightfall, and every step they took today was one less they'd have to face tomorrow. Despite their shortcut, they still had another half-day's travel before they would intersect with the path their clanmates had taken. Had they reached the crash site already? Were there other survivors? Was the ship intact enough to let them salvage parts and equipment? As far as he was concerned, salvage was even more important than finding mates.

The verexi had spun a web of lies to trick them into coming here. They'd claimed the entire project to create a fighting force was a failure, and the surviving subjects would be allowed to live out their lives on this planet, complete with everything they'd need to live comfortably.

Memories of what happened next made his fur stand on end. The scrawnies had no intention of letting their experiments live in peace. They'd planned to destroy the ship and claim it was an accident. Bysshe saved them. The android had risked deletion to uncover the verexis' plans and warn the fa'rel.

They'd broken free of the cargo hold and taken control of the ship's systems. Then they'd wound up crashing it onto the planet anyway because none of them had flight training. Since then, Risk had learned all he could from manuals and information Bysshe managed to extract from their dead ship's computers. If they ever found a working vessel, he was the only one who might be able to fly it.

So far, the only other ships to come to this place were full of mercenaries hired to kill them. Every time they got close to one, the surviving mercs flew away or the ship self-destructed.

The newly crashed ship was unlikely to ever fly

again, but if it had a shuttle and it was relatively intact? That could change everything.

The forest thinned out as they reached the first rise of hills. The ship had gone down on the far side, which meant tomorrow's trek would be all uphill. Their brothers had taken a longer route through flatter terrain, marking the trail as they went. It would be easier to carry salvaged parts and equipment that way, not to mention any surviving females.

All three of them scanned their surroundings, looking for a place to camp for the night. The sky was painted with colors as the sun set, adding intensity to the orange and yellow foliage and making it look as if the land around them was ablaze.

Sunsets were one of the many things he loved about his new life. The moon where they'd been imprisoned had been gray and almost lifeless thanks to the incredibly thin atmosphere. Squat, square buildings as bland as the landscape huddled underneath an atmospheric dome.

By comparison, their new home was a vibrant place, as beautiful as it was dangerous. The females would need protection from the local predators.

Fortunately for them, the fa'rel were more dangerous than anything else on this planet.

He liked the idea of having someone to protect—a soft, gentle female who would look at him the way Hope had looked at Menace. He didn't know the names for the emotions he'd seen in her expression, but he wanted them just the same.

Something glinted in the corner of his vision, and he turned to get a better look. What was that? A trick of the light? A reflection?

It took a few seconds for his brain to accept what he was looking at wasn't a hallucination. It was a ship!

He pointed to the metallic shape. "Tell me that's what I think it is."

His brothers turned to look.

"A ship!" Vengeance looked like he was about to sprint up the hill.

"It's some kind of vessel," Havoc agreed, still staring. "But how long has it been there? Bysshe said they only saw three escape pods on the scans, and this isn't anywhere near where the big ship went down."

Venge growled in frustration. "You're too fucking cautious."

"And you're both too focused on finding females. It's a ship. That means possible supplies and salvage," Risk said.

Havoc gave him a side-eyed look and scoffed. "You're hoping it can still fly. Aren't you?"

Risk tugged on one of his horns and shrugged. "Maybe. We should still check it out." He pointed at Venge. "But slowly. If females are around, charging in there will scare them. Especially if yours is the first face they see."

Venge bristled and growled. "You calling me ugly?"

Havoc laughed. "Not ugly, my brother. Terrifying."

"That's better," Vengeance bared his teeth at them and then spun on his heel and raced away.

"What happened to slow?" Risk called after him.

Havoc shook his head. "You know what he's like. If we don't hurry, he'll try to claim every female he finds."

Despite their talk of females, Risk wasn't the only one who drew his weapon as they approached. Vengeance held his largest blade, and Havoc had a short spear in one hand and a knife in the other. Risk left his blades sheathed but carried a bola he could use to entangle and immobilize whatever he threw it at.

The evening breeze shifted, bringing with it the unmistakable scent of cooked food. Risk inhaled and quickly determined it wasn't one meal but several. Holy hells, could another group of females actually be out here?

The three of them spread out, following the same pattern they used while hunting. Vengeance stayed in the lead while Havoc covered his flank, and Risk circled around behind.

He was naturally stealthy—a skill Rage and some of the others had encouraged him to practice. He was the only one of his clan-brothers to escape and return without ever being caught. He explored new areas, delivered messages to those in isolation, and met with Bysshe sometimes. The android was the only ally they'd had. He'd done what he could to help: relaying information, warnings, and food when he could. As far as the fa'rel were concerned, Bysshe was their blue-skinned clan-brother, despite his lack of horns and fur.

Vengeance lost patience and approached before Risk was in position. *Idiot.* The male was equal parts fearless and foolish.

His brother stepped into view of anyone inside the ship, his blade still in his hand. Vengeance took no more than two steps before a blaster pulse slammed into the ground by his feet.

"That's far enough." The voice was steady, firm, and clearly female.

Apparently, not all human females were helpless. Why hadn't anyone mentioned that?

Risk moved silently, using what little cover he had to stay hidden. He managed to reach a location with a good view of the situation, and what he saw made him want to curse. A female with hair the color of morning mist leaned out of the ship's entryway, a blaster in her hand with most of her body hidden.

Another armed female lay at the first one's feet, her blaster aimed at Havoc. Her face was hidden by the weapon she held in her small hands, but he caught a glimpse of dark hair with a touch of frost at the temples and a band of something silver sitting on her brow. Was it a weapon? A decoration? He had no idea.

Havoc raised his hands slightly and dropped his knives in a show of surrender. It might have worked, if only their brother had done the same.

He didn't. Vengeance still gripped his blade with both hands, the tip raised in anticipation of battle.

Risk uttered a low growl of frustration. So much for slow.

3

THE LAST FEW days had been full of firsts for Joy, and she hadn't enjoyed any of them. First time being attacked by a fellow crew member. Check.

First time evacuating from a crippled ship about to crash. Check.

First time stranded on an uninhabited planet. Check.

Now, she was pointing a weapon at a living being instead of a holographic target for the first time, and it sucked harder than a black hole. She didn't want to hurt anyone, but she would if necessary. Captain Perez had ordered her to take care of their guests, and she intended to do so.

The alien she aimed at was huge, horned, and covered in golden fur. Her job required her to recognize every race in the known galaxy, and the new arrivals weren't on her list. Were they native to this planet? More importantly. Were they hostile? The weapons they carried suggested they could be. Loris clearly assumed they were a threat, but the woman was a professional bodyguard with trust issues. Joy suspected Loris viewed *everyone* as a potential threat.

"Do you understand me?" Loris called out.

"We do," the one holding two knives said. "We have translators. I'm Havoc." He nodded toward the larger male. "That's Vengeance. You must be from the *Bountiful Harvest*."

Loris hissed in surprise and then whispered, "How the fuck does he know that?"

Joy answered without moving, her focus on the male, "Ask him."

"How do you know about the *Harvest*?" Loris asked.

A third male stepped into view at that moment, his empty hands held up and out. This alien was similar to the others, but his features were sharper, especially his cheekbones, and he didn't have a beard. None of them wore much in the way of clothing, either. Just a leather kilt that hung from their hips and some kind of protectors lashed to their lower legs. She was supposed to be watching Havoc, but she couldn't tear her gaze away from the nameless new arrival. He was the most beautiful being she'd ever seen.

"I am Risk. We met one of the other survivors from your ship—a female named Hope."

Relief flooded through her. There were other survivors! "Hope made it? Where is she?"

Risk looked at her and nodded, his amber eyes gleaming in the last rays of the setting sun. "We saw her this morning. Her escape pod came down much closer to our home. She was rescued by one of our brothers. We were on our way to the main crash site to assist when we saw your shuttle."

She made a decision at that moment and set her weapon down. They were here to help, not do harm.

Loris sighed and nudged her with the toe of her shoe. "You can't help yourself. Can you? You don't have a single distrustful bone in your body. Pick up the weapon, Joy. It could be a trick."

Joy considered that idea but then discarded it. A large part of her job was assessing someone's personality, needs, and desires so she could help them make a good match. She'd seen enough of these males to make a first assessment. They weren't a threat. At least, not to her or her companions.

"What else can you tell us? Were there other survivors? What about the *Harvest*? Did it land safely or crash?"

Risk flicked his fingers forward to indicate Loris

and her weapon. "Put down the blaster and we'll share what we know."

"You first," Loris said firmly.

Havoc and Risk looked at their empty hands and then turned to look at the one they'd called Vengeance. The big male still held his sword in front of him but now grinned broadly enough she could see he had fangs.

"For fuck's sake, Venge," Risk growled. "We talked about this."

"You talked. I wasn't listening," Vengeance said.

Joy couldn't help herself. She giggled. "You must be related. Only family bicker like that," she said.

Loris poked her with her toe again. "Stop laughing. We're trying to look intimidating."

"I think that ship has left orbit," Maddison said from her spot deeper inside the shuttle. She tried to sound calm, but Joy heard the crackle of tension in her voice. After all Maddison had endured in her life, the arrival of three large, aggressive males couldn't be easy for her to deal with.

"We are clan-brothers," Havoc confirmed. Then he dropped his voice to a low growl and snarled at Vengeance. "Disarm, brother. The hunt is over."

The hunt. The words sent a shiver down Joy's spine. If these aliens were the hunters, that made the three of them prey.

Vengeance held out one hand, palm raised, and returned his blade-sword thing to a sheath on his back. "I am disarmed, little warrior. Now it's your turn."

"Who does he think he's calling little?" Loris huffed, sounding a little flustered.

The bodyguard had a point. Loris was taller and heavier than most human women and quite a few human men, too.

Vengeance laughed and thumped his bare chest with a fist. "You are small compared to me. Tiny, but fierce."

Loris lowered her weapon. "I think you just insulted me and complimented me in the same sentence. Call me Loris." She pointed down and toward the back of the ship. "That's Joy, and Maddison is inside."

Risk looked around their meager camp, probably searching for somewhere to sit. Loris and Maddison had managed to drag over a stone and a partially rotted log to the fire pit they'd made, but that was it. The emergency shelter and supplies were set up on the other side of the ship. The wind tended to blow in the same direction, and they'd arranged their little camp to ensure the ship blocked most of it.

Not that Joy had seen most of the camp, yet. She'd been aboard the ship since landing here. Hooper's attack had done more than knock her out cold. Thanks to that lunatic, Joy had a mild concussion and a badly sprained ankle. They'd made the collective decision to treat her concussion with advanced meds from the first aid kit but to leave her ankle to heal on its own. They had no idea how long they'd be here and agreed to save their meager supplies for emergencies.

Joy had another issue to deal with, but she hadn't told her companions about it. Her implants weren't connecting to her coronet properly, and the distorted feedback gave her a constant headache and moments of blurred vision. Since none of them had the skills or equipment to fix it, she saw no reason to mention it at all. They had enough to deal with already.

If you want a place to sit, you'll have to find something yourselves," Joy told the three males.

"Why are there only two spots to sit when there are three of you?" Risk asked.

"Because one of us is injured and can't move around easily," Loris said before Joy could speak.

"Is it serious? Can we do anything to help?" Havoc asked.

"Is it you, little warrior? If it is, I will carry you to the fire and let you sit on my lap as we talk," Vengeance said with a cocky grin.

"It's nothing serious, and it's not me. And I told you to stop calling me that. My name is Loris, not little warrior."

Vengeance shrugged. "Your name is pretty, but I like my name for you better. And even if you are not hurt, my offer to carry you stands."

Loris tried to look stern, but Joy's sensors informed her the other woman's temperature had risen slightly, especially around her face and neck. No doubt about it, Loris was enjoying the brash alien's attention. Despite everything, Joy's love of matchmaking kicked in, and she started considering whether the two would be good together. They certainly had chemistry, despite the significant difference in age. All three women were in their late forties or older while the aliens were fit, virile, and clearly in their prime. Lucky Loris. She'd have to do what she could to help their chemistry along. It was what she did, after all, and making matches for others was as close as she'd ever get to finding love herself.

It took only a few minutes to organize seating and turn on the solar-powered lanterns they'd found among the emergency supplies. The males quickly accepted their offer of food, and Maddison brought out a selection of self-heating meal packs for them before joining Loris near the fire. Joy stayed where she was. The doorway was not the most comfortable spot, but the position allowed her to join in without putting strain on her still-healing ankle.

Risk didn't take his eyes off her for more than a few seconds while they arranged things. She knew that because no matter how hard she tried to look anywhere else, her gaze—or at least her electronic version of it— kept returning to him. He moved with the grace of a predator despite his large size, and his lack of clothing gave her a tantalizing view of powerful muscles flowing under his tawny fur. The bag and some of the equipment he'd carried had been set aside, leaving him wearing nothing but a short leather kilt and the daggers still bound to his biceps by strips of leather. In many ways he looked like a human male, only built on a bigger scale. She noticed some marked differences, though. The horns for one. They curved up and back from his face before arcing down to taper into points by his ears.

His face and back were marked with dark stripes that only added to the sense of danger that all three aliens exuded. She wanted to know more about them but only after they'd shared what they knew about the other survivors.

Once the others were seated, Risk looked at her. "You're the injured one?"

She pointed toward her foot. "I sprained my ankle, and it hasn't fully healed yet. I'm trying to stay off it as much as I can. I'll be fine in a few more days. Now, please, tell us about the others."

Havoc took over the conversation, telling them what he knew. It wasn't as much information as she'd hoped for, but she took some comfort in the knowledge that Hope, Clarissa, and Bella were alive and well.

They didn't have any news about the *Harvest*. But other members of their clan were on their way to the crash site and would take care of any survivors they found. It would be days before they knew more, so Joy did her best to put her worries aside. She couldn't do anything to change the outcome.

"Why are the three of you so far from the main ship?" Havoc asked.

"And can this shuttle still fly?" Risk added.

"And what made the ship crash at all?" Vengeance asked.

Loris answered Vengeance's question first. "We had engine trouble, fell out of hyperspace, and were immediately attacked. At least, that's the impression I got when we reached the bridge."

All three males nodded.

"We were right. The scrawnies have this place well-guarded," Havoc said.

"Who are the scrawnies?" Maddison spoke for the first time.

"The verexi," Havoc clarified. "We have our own name for the scrawny bastards."

"They do that? Why?" Loris asked.

Havoc nodded. "I'm certain of it. They don't want anyone coming here until they eradicate us."

"Eradicate you?" Loris stiffened. "Why?"

Vengeance snorted. "Because we're a mistake they want to erase from existence. This is a prison planet, little warrior. We were sent here to die. We survived, and that's a problem for the scrawnies—one they want to correct."

Joy's stomach twisted. "The verexi are still trying to kill you even though you can't leave this place?"

"They are," Risk stated, his tone edged in ice. "And if they find out you survived, they'll kill you, too."

Shit. They'd activated the distress beacon days ago and had a recorded message going out on the ship's comms every hour. The shuttle didn't have the ability to send messages long distances, but anyone in the system would be able to receive it. She turned to Loris. "We have to shut down the beacon and the radio right now!"

All three males shot to their feet. "You've had a beacon going all this time?" Risk demanded.

"We didn't know!" Maddison stammered. "Please. We wouldn't have done it if we knew it would endanger you."

Loris sprinted back to the ship, arriving at the same time Joy managed to get to her feet. She moved out of the other woman's way, pressing herself against the nearest wall as Loris ran to the cockpit to shut down all outgoing transmissions.

"Done!" Loris called out less than a minute later.

Joy noticed that all three males had gathered up their equipment and now stood back to back, their eyes scanning ground and sky for any sign of danger.

"Can this ship fly?" Risk asked again.

"No. The autopilot brought us down on its own. Once we were down, it locked us out of the flight controls," Joy said.

"It's a security feature to prevent theft. Only the command crew know the codes." Loris sighed. "And the ones the captain gave me as we left don't work."

Risk nodded once and turned to the others. "I will stay. The shuttle is too valuable to abandon."

"We'll take the females to safety and be back as soon as we can," Havoc said.

"Bring Strife and Bysshe, if he's able. If I can't access the flight systems, maybe one of them can."

Vengeance growled in what she thought was frustration. "I should stay, too. They will come."

"No. The females need your protection." Risk bared his teeth. "I don't."

Joy piped up. "The females would like a say in what happens next. This isn't only your decision."

"Damn right it's not!" Loris called out from the cockpit.

Vengeance muttered something under his breath and stalked toward the ship. Joy considered blocking his path but opted to let Loris deal with it.

Still a warning seemed fair. "Loris, you've got incoming."

"Venge..." Havoc growled the male's name in warning.

Maddison's eyes went wide. "Don't let him hurt her!"

"He won't." Risk sounded amused. "She's safer with him than anyone else in the galaxy."

Joy caught his meaning, but Maddison didn't.

"What? Why?" Maddison asked.

She understood Maddison's fear but didn't share the feeling. She knew Risk and his friends represented their best chance of surviving, and clearly something was developing between Vengeance and Loris.

Joy hopped backward to make room for Vengeance. Once he'd passed, she limped back to the door and started to make her way down the ramp. Part way down she lost her balance.

"Ack!" she yelped and flailed her arms in a desperate attempt to stay upright.

She braced for a painful impact, only to be caught mid-fall. Strong arms cradled her against a very broad, naked chest. A wave of desire crashed over her, drowning her common sense and leaving her drunk with desire.

"I've got you," Risk said, his voice a low rumble she felt as well as heard.

Without thinking, she wrapped one arm around his neck. "Or maybe I've got you."

Had she really said something that cheesy? What the hell was wrong with her?

Risk stared down at her for several long seconds before he spoke again. "What did you do to me, female? I burn."

Holy novas, was he feeling the same rush of desire as her? How was that even possible? "I don't know. I mean, I didn't do anything," she said in a breathy rush.

He growled softly and lowered his head until his lips were almost touching hers. He drew in a deep lungful of air and moved again, this time letting his nose brush her cheek and then her hair. "You," he whispered, a note of wonder in his voice.

She stroked the back of his neck, feeling the velvety softness of his fur beneath her fingers.

He shivered as she touched him, his next breath mingled with a groan that made her heart race. He wanted her. She could feel it. Heat coursed through her veins and need like she'd never known ignited deep in her core.

"Joy? Are you okay?" Maddison's question cut through the fog of lust clouding her mind.

"I'm fine. Just, uh, a little unsteady. Risk was making sure I didn't trip again."

Risk grumbled so softly only she could hear him. "That's *not* what I was doing."

"Me either," she whispered back. "Hold that thought?"

"I'd rather hold you."

Risk walked down the ramp and back to the circle of seats that ringed the firepit with her still in his arms.

"You can put me down now," she prompted.

"No. I think Venge had the right idea. I'll sit and you can rest in my lap. You'll be more comfortable that way."

Maddison looked startled and slightly panicked. "Joy?"

"I'm fine. Risk isn't going to hurt me. They're just bossy."

As if to prove her point, Loris yelled from inside the ship. "What the hell? No! Put me down!"

A few seconds later, Vengeance reappeared with Loris slung over his shoulder. She was smacking his back with open hands and swearing a blue streak as he carried her out of the ship.

"This one is mine," he announced.

"The hell I am! Put. Me. Down!"

Havoc shook his head and glanced over at Maddison. "I guess this means you're with me."

"What? No! I'm not with anyone. I mean, I wasn't on this cruise looking for a mate. I own the *Harvest*. That's all."

"I meant for the journey back to our home." Havoc surprised Joy by walking over to Maddison and crouching down in front of her, his hands lifted, palms up. "You aren't safe here. None of us are. We need to leave before the scrawnies send someone to investigate."

"But what if it's a rescue party?"

Loris kicked and wriggled until Vengeance set her down. "No one is coming to rescue us, Maddison. We're deep in verexi territory. I don't know how we got here or what went wrong, but we need to make the best of it."

She turned and glared at Vengeance. "And no, that was not me agreeing to anything. I'm just being practical."

"You do that. I am patient. Eventually you'll see I am right." The big male grinned at Loris. "You are mine."

Risk lowered his head to whisper in Joy's ear, "And you are mine."

Then he raised his head and announced, "Joy is injured and cannot walk, so she will stay with me."

"But what about the verexi?" Maddison demanded. "You said it wasn't safe to stay here."

"The ship is too valuable to leave behind. I will keep it and Joy safe," Risk said firmly.

Havoc spoke next, "Maddison and Loris. You have five minutes to pack food, water, and clothing. Then we must go."

Loris bristled at his tone but didn't argue. Maddison glanced over to her bodyguard. Loris flashed a quick series of hand signals, and Maddison gave the slightest of nods.

Joy gave them both what she hoped was an encouraging smile and waved the other women off. "Go. Find the other survivors. Stay safe."

"But what about you?" Maddison asked.

"I'll be fine," she said. And she believed it. *Mostly.*

Risk would safeguard her from the verexi and anything else on this planet. If his price for that protection was what she thought it was... she was more than happy to oblige. It had been too long since any male showed her more than a second of interest.

4

RISK HAD GONE on this hunt hoping to find a ship he could fly or a female to claim. Now he had both and no idea what the hell to do next.

No, that wasn't true. He *wanted* to peel Joy out of her clothes, lay her down in the grass, and fuck her until every living thing in the area knew his name. With every breath, he drew in more of her intoxicating scent, and he reveled in the way her soft, curvy body pressed against his. He'd never held a female before. The pleasure bots provided by the verexi were the closest he'd ever been to one. The bots were a tool he'd gladly used to ease his frustrations and boredom, but that was all they'd been. Joy was something else completely. She was *his* female.

It didn't matter that he couldn't explain how he knew she belonged to him. It was a fact. It happened the moment he'd caught her and stopped her fall. Touching her was like being electrocuted, only instead of pain he felt only raw need and a strange sense of completeness, like he had found a piece of himself he hadn't known was missing. This had to be what the others had experienced when they found their females.

When the time came, it wasn't easy to help Joy sit down and then leave her to see his brothers off.

Vengeance took a blaster from his pack and handed it to him. "You will need this more than I will."

Both he and Havoc stared at the weapon. Then Havoc reached over and cuffed the back of Vengeance's head. "You took one of the weapons from the cache? That's forbidden!"

The big male just shrugged and gave a wry grin. "You think I was the only one? Nearly half the stash was missing when I got there."

"Bysshe will skin you all alive and recycle your hides to make more of those jumpsuits he likes," Havoc muttered.

"He will have to catch us first." Vengeance bared his teeth and laughed. "Keep the blaster. You can use it to protect your female. Havoc and I will vanish into the woods soon. The mercenaries won't find us. They will come for you and this ship."

Risk held up the weapon. "And I will be waiting for them. The ship is ours. They can't have it."

"The ship or the female?" Havoc asked.

"Both." Risk had to hold back a snarl. If they even looked at Joy, they'd regret it. He usually found it easy to get along with his clanmates, but not now. Once he and Joy were marked as mates the same way Menace and Hope had been... maybe. But why hadn't it happened yet? No one had mentioned a timeframe.

Fuck. He should have asked more questions, but he'd been more interested in finding out about the ship. He'd expected all the females to be claimed by the time they caught up.

Vengeance barked out a laugh. "I feel the same about my little warrior. *Mine.*" He stressed the last word and added a low growl at the end.

Havoc scrubbed a hand through his beard and looked thoughtful. "I don't know if Maddison is mine... but she needs my protection. She is too gentle for this world." He chuckled. "And for me."

Risk nodded. He'd seen the way that female flinched and watched with wary eyes. She had been hurt by someone. Badly. He knew the signs because all the fa'rel had been tortured and abused by the verexi. He'd seen that look in his brothers' eyes too often not to recognize it.

The three of them looked at each other and nodded once. The sooner they went their separate ways, the better it would be for all of them. Only one thing was left to say. Risk bowed his head, and the others did the same. The knocked their horns together and spoke what had become their ritual phrase since gaining their freedom. "Good hunting, my brothers."

He didn't wait to see them leave. It was best if he didn't know which paths they took or where they planned to stop for the night. He needed to stay focused on his own mission... protecting his female.

He turned to find Joy watching him. She had her lower lip caught between her teeth and her hands clasped firmly in her lap. She seemed worried. But why?

"We should talk," she said before he could say anything.

"About what?" He crouched in front of her, eager to get a better look at her face.

That's when he saw the scars. Both eyes and part of her cheeks were marked with raised, uneven skin. The marks were old and faded, but now he was paying attention, they were obvious.

Joy laughed, and the sound made his heart swell and his cock get even harder. This little female would be the death of him if he didn't get to fuck her soon. This was insanity... but he didn't care.

"My face." She reached up to touch a spot beneath her eye.

"You have scars. So do I." He placed his hand over

her smaller one. "They mark you as a survivor. You're strong and determined. That's good."

She shook her head. "That's not all they indicate. We are in a difficult situation, and you need to know this, so I'll be blunt. I'm blind, Risk."

He rocked back on his heels in surprise. "You can't see? But you were aiming a weapon earlier." The idea of her shooting without being able to see confounded him. So did the fact she was alive at all. The verexi ruthlessly culled any member of their species who did not meet certain criteria. Humans clearly didn't share that mentality, which was a point in their favor.

"I can see, just not the same way you do. The metal band on my head has sensors embedded in it, and it sends the information to my brain through connection points in my skull." She pulled her hand out from beneath his and turned her face away from him. "I'm sorry."

Now he was even more confused. "Why are you sorry? For what?"

Joy raised her hands in a meek gesture. "Because I'm broken. No male wants a broken female." Her lips twitched, but the smile seemed bitter and sad. "Believe me. I know. That was my job on the ship. I was the one who tried to make good matches between the women and the males who signed up to meet them."

"That is a job? Why? What kind of male needs

help choosing a mate?" Was the galaxy filled with idiots? Risk suspected that was the case.

His questions made her laugh. "The average male needs a lot of help, or I would be in another line of work."

"Then I am not average. I don't need assistance to decide what I want." He caught her chin in his hand and gently drew her head back so she faced him. Now she'd told him, he could see that her eyes didn't focus on him the way they should. She would be helpless if the machine she used broke down, but that only made him more determined to protect her. She *needed* him, and he liked the way that felt.

"You think you do, but this might just be pheromones. Or hormones. Or well...I don't know what else but neither of us can be sure of anything right now. I mean, apart from the obvious."

Her cheeks heated beneath his fingers, and she tried to turn away again. He didn't allow it. She needed to understand.

"I am sure. You belong to me, now. I feel it here." He thumped a fist to his chest. "And here." He pointed to his groin. "My brothers found their females and bonded with them. We will do the same."

"You mean they claimed the women and had sex with them. That's not the same thing." Her brow scrunched up in a delightful way as she continued talking. "Not that I'm saying sex is bad. Or that us having sex would be bad. It would probably be amazing."

"It *will* be amazing. The pleasure bots the verexi provided us were instructional models. I know how to make a female scream with pleasure, and I will prove it to you very soon."

"Oh!" Her voice was breathy and higher pitched than normal. He couldn't tell if that was good or bad. He'd never spoken to another species before today, and the only other female he'd ever seen was Menace's mate.

"That's uh. That's good to know. But it's not what I meant." Joy chewed on her lip for several seconds before continuing. "I'm saying I don't expect you to stay with me forever. If whatever this is fizzles out, we go our separate ways. No harm, no regrets."

Risk growled, frustrated and angry at the idea of her leaving him. "You will stay with me."

"For now, yes. I'm just saying that if you change your mind, it's okay. I understand."

"No, you don't." He pointed to the twin moons rising in the night sky. "Do you see those moons? They travel together. Always. That is us."

She raised her head to look in the direction he pointed. "Those are space rocks. Gravity and physics keep them in place. People are more complicated.

We're strangers to each other. There's no way to know how we'll interact yet."

"I know a way." Talking about this wasn't working, so he stopped trying to explain. There'd be time for conversation later. He moved toward her, shifting from a crouch to kneel at her feet as one hand wrapped around her waist. He cupped the back of her head with his other hand, careful not to jostle the metal band he thought of as her crown.

Joy uttered a soft gasp but didn't pull away. *Good.* Though the thought of chasing this little female through the forest and tumbling her to the ground appealed to him, too.

A fresh wave of lust crashed over him, and he stopped thinking about anything but the female in front of him. His lips slanted over hers, offering him his first taste. Her mouth was warm, her lips soft as they parted beneath his, inviting him deeper.

Nothing in his life compared to the pleasure he felt as he twined his tongue with hers, every touch making him crave her even more.

She shivered and moaned, the sound buzzing against his lips. It was the most beautiful sound he'd ever heard in the world. He was already giving her pleasure and they had only just started. He wanted to know what other noises she'd make when he was buried balls deep inside her, his cock swollen so they were locked together.

Then she'd understand who she belonged to.

She stroked his chest and shoulders as they kissed, her soft hands leaving trails of fire everywhere she touched. Then her hands moved up his neck and into his hair. She pulled him closer and kissed him back, her legs parting so he could move between them.

Now his cock was achingly close to her pussy, and it was all he could do not to pull her into his arms and thrust himself against her soft body. He wanted to fuck her here and now, but it wasn't safe. Not when the enemy might appear at any moment.

Fuck. The enemy. Had he lost so much of his mind he'd forgotten about the danger? He needed to protect Joy and the ship. To do that...

He struggled to find the willpower to raise his head and break their kiss, but he managed it.

"Inside. We need to get inside the ship," he said.

Joy frowned. "But the tent is more comfortable."

"The shelter is bright yellow and likely painted with elements that will make it light up like a beacon if the area is scanned. It's also made of fabric. Cloth is not known for its resistance to blaster fire." He pointed to the shuttle. "The hull will hold out longer."

Her expression shifted from confused to

concerned. "You really think they'll come here and try to kill us?"

"I do. The scrawnies will have told their own version of events to the other species. They cannot allow the truth to come out. They want all evidence of their experiments destroyed. *We* are the evidence. One day, we will escape this planet and share the truth with the others."

"That's why you want the shuttle," she said.

It wasn't a question. She was smart enough to understand without further explanation.

"Yes. Now, we are going inside." He rose to his feet and then gathered her into his arms. "We have too much to do."

"You mean fixing the shuttle? I told you I'm not part of the flight crew. I'm not going to be much help there."

"That is one of the things I meant. First, though, we get naked and fuck. Maybe then I will get back enough of my mind to fix the shuttle." He grinned down at her. "Right now, you are all I can think about."

"There's not a lot of room to lie down in there," she said.

"Lying down is optional. Fucking you is not. We'll manage."

To his delight, she laughed and threw her arms around his neck. "Yes, I guess we will."

5

JOY STOPPED TRYING to make sense of her situation and decided to enjoy the madness. Risk hadn't been deterred by her blindness, her scars, or her lack of knowledge about shuttle operations. She'd been honest about all her shortcomings, and he hadn't cared about any of it. For the first time since her accident, she felt whole. It couldn't last, but that was fine. She'd just enjoy the feeling for as long as she could. She gave the same advice to the guests who let their self-doubt get in the way of a chance at happiness. Sometimes, you needed to let go.

Risk's long legs and hurried pace brought them inside the ship in a matter of seconds. The interior wasn't much to look at. Storage was in the tail of the shuttle along with the door and a closet-sized enclosure that could be sealed to form an airlock. Toward the front was a small cabin area with an even smaller cockpit beyond that. The command shuttle was exactly what its name implied—a shuttle intended to carry a ship's command staff short distances.

Her self-appointed protector looked around with interest. "This will do." Then he turned with her still in his arms and pressed the switch that closed and sealed the door.

She wasn't sure she agreed with his assessment. Risk was so tall his horns nearly touched the ceiling, and he'd have to walk sideways to fit down the aisle that ran between the four seats. Each side had two chairs facing each other with a pullout table that could be set up between them. Arranged properly, they made two long but narrow beds. Since she was the only one living aboard, she'd left one side as a bed and used the other for meals and to read. There wasn't much else to do.

The remains of her dinner were still on the table. They were eating the self-heating meals from the emergency supplies, but the shuttle had a small, simple galley near the storage area that was stocked with several kinds of instant drinks and other snacks. Tonight, she'd indulged herself with a small container of chocolate pudding. It was so good she'd eaten half of it before she'd finished the main entrée. She'd had to abandon the meal when Loris announced they had company, and they'd scrambled to arm themselves and get into position.

It was hard to believe that all happened just an hour or so ago. Things were moving fast.

As if to prove her point, Risk reached out with one hand as if he planned to sweep everything off the table.

"Wait! Not the pudding. That's too good to waste." She squirmed and tried to grab his arm before he did the unthinkable.

To her relief, he stopped. "What is pudding?"

"A sweet dessert. That one is chocolate flavor, and it's delicious."

The look on Risk's face told her he had no idea how important chocolate was. Hell, it was right up there with coffee, and fortunes were made every day by anyone who figured out a way to grow either crop and get the product to market.

"It is important to you?"

His question surprised her. "I like chocolate, and it's the last on board. After it's gone, that's it."

His amber eyes gleamed as he carefully picked up the container and handed it to her. "Show me."

He hadn't picked up the spoon, but she'd make do without one. She stuck her finger into the pudding, withdrew it, and raised her dessert-laden digit to his mouth. "You'll see. Unless you are allergic to chocolate. In which case maybe you shouldn't—

He didn't wait for her to finish. He had her finger in his mouth that same second, sucking the creamy substance off her skin. It was one of the most erotic things she'd ever experienced. A rush of desire slammed into her, and all she could think about was the heat of his mouth and the intensity of his focus.

His tongue lapped at her skin, and she had to bite back a moan. Then she realized she had no reason to hide what she felt.

Risk's eyes widened as he got his first taste of chocolate.

"Good!" he said, managing the word without releasing her finger.

"See? I told you. If you put me down I'll put it away and we can..." she trailed off. "Uh, see to things that need doing."

It was the lamest thing she'd ever said, but Risk didn't seem to mind.

"Those things will happen right now, but the pudding stays. I want more of it."

"Whatever you want."

He laughed and she withdrew her hand. "The pudding is good. But I want *you*."

He knocked the rest of her meal to the floor and set her down on the table with her legs dangling over the edge.

She carefully set the pudding down on the table

and tried to remember to breathe as he unfastened the buckles holding the leather kilt in place and let it drop to the floor.

Holy nukes and fucking novas, how was it he looked even bigger now he was naked? Unlike most of his body, his cock was bare skin, which allowed her to see every bit of its thick length and multiple ridges.

If more like him were in the galaxy, they really needed to start arranging matchmaking tours with this species...

The thought made her smile, but it also brought a stab of jealousy. If that happened, Risk was not allowed to take part. He was *hers*, dammit.

She ignored that train of thought before it took her somewhere she wasn't ready to go. It was time to seize the moment. Or in this case...

Joy grabbed hold of Risk's curved horns and used them to pull him toward her. She parted her legs to make room for him, putting them back in to a position similar to the one they'd been in outside.

If he'd resisted, she wouldn't have been able to move him at all, but he didn't fight her. In fact, he grinned as he closed the distance between them.

She kissed *him* this time, slipping her tongue into his mouth to dance with his. He tasted of chocolate now, and part of her brain decided he was now her favorite dessert. She smiled again as she kissed him, so giddy with the pleasure of this unexpected liaison she wanted to throw back her head and laugh.

Joy explored as much of him as she could reach, stroking his fur-covered body and marveling at the muscles that bunched and shifted beneath her hands. She'd coached so many women through interspecies dating situations, but she'd never had a nonhuman lover. Not until now.

"You wear too many clothes," he complained without raising his lips from hers for longer than it took to speak.

She had to wait until the next pause to answer him. "Most humans wear several layers of clothing for warmth and to protect our skin from injury."

"I will keep you warm, little moon." A second later she felt a tug on her shirt followed by the sound of tearing fabric. A waft of cool air hit her skin, and she finally realized what he'd done.

"You ripped my shirt! It's the only one I have. Don't you dare rip my pants or I'll have to wander around completely naked."

The look he gave her was so hot she swore her visual sensors marked a rise in the air temperature. "I'd like that."

"I'm not sure I would." The last thing she wanted to do was wander around a hostile planet with her aging assets on display. Her stretch marks and sagging body bits weren't things she wanted anyone and everyone to see. Not to mention that without protection from the thorns and thick underbrush in the woods, she'd quickly be so marked up it would look like she'd been attacked by a swarm of rabid kittens.

He cocked his head to one side. "Why not?"

She could have explained her thinking but decided to go with the nuclear option, the one that would end this conversation immediately. "Do you really want me to be naked around your clan-brothers?"

Boom. Risk snarled and bared his teeth. "No!"

"Then help me take my pants off without tearing them."

She left the tattered remains of her shirt on while they worked together to ease her out of pants and shoes without hurting her ankle or sending her tumbling off the table. A sexy striptease this was not, but Risk didn't seem to mind. In fact, he was surprisingly gentle.

"You are not naked yet." He grumbled as he stood and tossed her pants down the aisle. "Why are you still wearing this?"

As tempting as it was to say something flippant to deflect his question and get to the good stuff, she didn't. She needed to be honest. "I'm worried that once you see me naked you won't want me anymore. I'm older than you, Risk. A *lot* older. You're young and clearly in the prime of your life. My prime has come and gone."

His amber eyes widened, and his handsome face fell into an expression of utter confusion. "Why wouldn't I want you?"

Fucking hell. How could she explain without making this whole situation worse? "Uh, because. Well, you're all muscle and strength. I'm not. I'm chubby and my skin has marks from age and gravity." She touched her temple. "My hair is turning gray, too. And not just the hair on my head." Fuck again. Had she really just said that?

"I have more than one color of hair, and I have scars. What does it matter?" He touched her cheek with almost reverential care.

"Because, uh. Well, it matters to the males of many species. I thought it might matter to yours, too."

He snorted. "These are the same males who need help finding a mate. I am nothing like them. The fa'rel aren't a species. We're experiments. The verexi created us to be their soldiers and tried to terminate us when they failed to make us compliant."

She laughed. "You're right. You are nothing like any other male I've ever met." Then more of what he'd said sank in. "Wait, you said you're called the fa'rel? Why does that name sound familiar?"

"I don't know." He leaned in and kissed the corner of her mouth. "And right now, I don't care. You talk too much, little moon."

He tugged the remains of her shirt away from her body and dropped it on the floor. "We'll talk later. Now, I want to see you." He grinned. "And then I want to taste you."

She shivered in anticipation. "And then?" she asked.

"And then I am going to fuck you until we are both too exhausted to continue."

As far as she was concerned, that sounded like the best plan she'd ever heard. "Yes, please."

His smile turned utterly wicked as he caught hold of her shirt and tugged it away. She had to let go of him to get her arms out of the sleeves. The moment she was untangled, he tossed the tattered fabric aside and then raked his gaze down her body like a starving man looking at an all-you-can-eat buffet.

No man had ever looked at her that way before, and it made her toes curl in anticipation of what might happen next.

"Pudding," he said and held out a hand.

"What? Oh, right. She twisted around and managed to pick up the requested container. He took it from her and then raised a finger and tipped it in her direction. "Do. Not. Move."

"I won't." She reached for him, but he leaned back far enough to stay out of reach. "Not yet. It's my turn first."

"Your turn?" The last word came out as more of a squeak as Risk dipped his finger into the dessert and then proceeded to paint her body with the contents. Cool, slippery trails of chocolate crisscrossed her breasts and circled her nipples while she did her best not to move. Something told her that now was not the time to test the limits of Risk's patience.

Once he seemed satisfied, he stood back and admired his handiwork... or her. She couldn't tell which.

"Beautiful," he murmured.

"And sticky," she said.

"Not for long." He moved again, this time bending down to swipe his tongue along the path of chocolate he'd made. The heat of his mouth was a shocking contrast after the coolness of the pudding. She gasped, arching toward him as he continued to feast on her body.

Her hands were on his horns before she realized she'd moved them, but he didn't complain. She used them to help her keep her balance as he coaxed her backward, his hand in the small of her back.

He devoured her inch by inch, working his way lower until his lips nuzzled the soft bulge of her belly. He paused, pressed his face in close, and then inhaled deeply. "I think you smell even better than the dessert. Do you taste better, too?"

She opened her mouth to answer him, but before she could think of anything to say, he pressed two pudding-covered fingers to the seam of her pussy and then slid them inside.

A jolt of raw desire sizzled through her body, making her back arch and her legs move farther apart. She moaned and let her head fall back and her eyes close. She could still see, of course. Her coronet of sensors still fed visual data into her brain, but over the years she'd learned how to ignore that input for short periods. Right now, her vision wasn't the sense she wanted to focus on.

Risk guided her back even further until she was lying flat on the table, her head tilting up slightly as it rested on the bulkhead behind her.

He kissed her once, his lips tasting of chocolate and desire. She raised her head to kiss him back, but he pulled away, blazing a trail of kisses down her body. His fingers moved inside her folds, exploring and stroking until he found the bundle of nerves within their swollen hood of flesh.

When he touched her clit, she shivered and arched her hips, making it clear she liked that and wanted more.

"Yes?" he asked, working his callused fingertips over the spot.

"Oh, yes. More. Please."

He grinned. "I like it when you say please."

"If you keep doing that, I'm likely to make all sorts of noises." She could hardly believe the words coming out of her mouth. She wasn't one to talk during sex. Her partners had never wanted her to say or do anything really.

Risk was different. Stars and novas was he ever.

"Good." He kissed his way down one thigh, his fangs grazing her sensitive skin as he slowly drew her legs up over his shoulders and lowered his head to the seam of her sex. His breath fanned over her damp skin, and for several long seconds, she waited for him to make contact.

Just as she was about to squirm in protest, something cool and wet touched her thigh and she realized he'd painted more of the pudding on her skin. She shivered in need and then loosed a low moan of pure rapture as he placed an open-mouthed kiss on her thigh, licking and sucking his way up to the apex of her thighs. This time he kept going, his wicked mouth moving over the lips of her pussy and teasing her until she was panting.

She tugged on his horns, pulling him in close as she raised her hips off the table and ground herself against his mouth. Her clit throbbed in time to her pounding heart as he stroked it again and again with his fingers. Then his tongue slid between her folds and she was lost to everything but the pleasure of his touch.

Lust crackled through her veins and sent sparks of desire dancing across her skin. A maelstrom of pure need roared around her as Risk laid claim to her body with a raw passion she couldn't get enough of.

He devoured her as she writhed and gasped beneath him, every flick of his tongue and touch of his fingers driving her farther out of her mind. He sucked on her clit, growling in approval as she arched and cried his name.

She guided him with her body, encouraged him with every sound she made, and loved every second of it. When he slipped a finger inside her channel, her walls flexed, gripping him tightly.

Risk uttered a sound somewhere between a growl and a groan and pressed his finger deeper, stretching her slowly as he added a second finger.

When she gasped, he raised his head to look at her. "You are so tight and tiny. I don't want to hurt you."

Part of her mind came back when she heard the concern in his lust-roughened voice. "You won't. But you're so big, it might be best if you give me a chance to stretch first." She managed a soft breathy laugh. "It has been a very long time since I used those muscles."

"It's been a long time for me, too." He bent his head and returned to nibbling and sucking on her throbbing clit while his fingers fucked her with slow strokes that left her needing more.

Her grip on his horns tightened, and she used the leverage to raise her hips off the table, trying for more contact, more pleasure, more of *everything*. She was near her breaking point when Risk curled his fingers slightly, hitting the perfect spot. She came apart like shattered crystal, exploding into a mind-stealing orgasm. She screamed his name, filling the cabin with the sounds of her pleasure.

She was still trembling when he raised his head again, withdrawing his fingers to swipe at his mouth with the back of his hand. His lips were smeared with chocolate, and she acted on impulse, sitting up while pulling him toward her so she could kiss him again.

His scent was stronger now, filling her nose with a blend of musk and spices she couldn't name but loved anyway. Then her mouth found his, and the taste of sex and chocolate exploded on her tongue.

He gripped her hip in one hand and positioned his cock at her entrance with the other. He moved the thick crown back and forth across her flesh until her toes curled and her blood felt like molten gold flowing through her veins. She had never wanted anyone the way she wanted Risk.

When he entered her, she groaned into his mouth, feeling every thick, ridged inch of his length. She forgot about her injured ankle and the hard surface of the table. Her world shrank down to one thing and one thing only—him.

The silky fur of his chest caressed her nipples as they came together, every touch pouring more rocket fuel on the flames of desire already burning her from the inside out.

Risk made a noise she thought was a growl. But then she felt the deep vibrations coming from his chest and realized he was... purring?

Fucking hell, her lover purred. It was the sexiest sound she'd ever heard.

"You are mine now," he murmured as he buried himself balls deep inside her. "Always mine."

She should have argued with him and reminded him this might not be forever, but she didn't want to say it. Hell, she didn't want to believe it. Whatever this was, she wanted it to last.

His purr deepened. "Say it," he demanded as he rocked his hips back and then forward again, using the ridges to stroke her inner walls and take her to the brink again.

"Always yours," the words fell from her lips.

He roared in triumph, and she laughed as a sense of pure joy swept over her, twining itself around her passion to form one perfect moment she'd never forget.

Then her mind shut down as their mutual need took control.

He powered into her, every thrust filling her impossibly full. They were linked in every way: hands gripping, mouths mated, tongues dancing, bodies pressing together.

She didn't know how long they stayed like that, chasing each other up mountains of pleasure. It could have been minutes, or hours, but eventually she reached her peak and came again. This time, his mouth captured her cries as she came, his arms wrapped around her to hold her tightly as she shuddered and gasped.

He reached his end a few strokes later, his orgasm breaking like waves on a rocky shore. It was impossibly, wonderfully perfect. But then somehow, it got better.

Risk's cock swelled inside her, locking the two of them together and triggering another series of orgasmic tremors to roll through her body.

Holy nukes and novas. If this was what the other women had experienced, no wonder they'd agreed to mate these males. They might look a little like devils, but they fucked like gods.

She was still lost in a lust-infused fog when Risk snarled and reared up, his hands swatting at his chest like something had burned him.

His expression went from fury to confusion as he looked down and patted his chest with both hands.

"What's wrong? What happened?" Her sensors detected a strange increase in temperature, but she could only get a partial impression because his big hands blocked her view.

"It burned," he said as she sat up and tugged at his hands so she could get a better look. The motion reminded her that they were still locked together with the thick base of his cock pressed against her inner walls, triggering another aftershock of pleasure.

"What burned you?"

"I don't know, but it stopped. Now, I have these." He scowled and poked at two sets of parallel black lines that crisscrossed his chest. Four lines in each set, intersecting over his breast bone.

"Those weren't there before."

She reached for them and then froze as the skin on her wrists tingled. The feeling intensified, and her sensors detected yet another heat spike. This time, though, she saw the pattern more clearly. Four lines running in parallel, crossing over the center of her wrist. It was the same as Risk's, only smaller and in a different location.

"I don't understand. What is this? Why?" She had so many questions crowding her head she couldn't decide where to start.

Risk looked from his chest to her wrists. His eyes widened, and then he threw back his head and roared. The sound was deafening in the small space, especially when the two of them were still locked together.

She still had no idea what the marks were or what they meant, but clearly Risk did, and he was more than pleased about them.

Joy touched her hand to his marks and then saw something new about the pattern. She splayed out her fingers and compared. Yes. She was right. The marks looked like scratches. Two sets of claw marks crossing Risk's chest diagonally from each shoulder.

"I still don't understand," she reminded her lover. That wasn't true, though. She already had an inkling what the marks meant and why he was so happy about them.

"We are mates. These markings appeared on the others too. It confirms what I already knew, little moon." He grinned and flashed his fangs. "You are mine."

She raised her wrist to show off her new marks. "Then this means something else, too." She laughed as a sense of wonder and hope suffused her heart and soul. "You are mine, Risk of the fa'rel."

He wrapped his arms around her and grinned like a cat with a vat full of cream. "That is acceptable. Only you must remember that I claimed you first."

6

————

Nothing could have prepared Risk for this moment. He was crammed between the flight chairs of a fully functional shuttle cockpit, trying to rewire the console to get around the lockout setting while his beautiful and very naked female sat on a blanket near his feet and handed him tools.

"You sure you don't need to take a break? That can't be comfortable."

He chuckled. "It isn't, but if I climb out of here I'm not sure I'll be able to get back in again."

His back, shoulders, and arms ached, but it wasn't the first time he'd been uncomfortable. It was, however, the first time someone else had expressed concern about him. His brothers cared, but the only time they spoke about feelings and supporting each other was after consuming too much of Bysshe's fruit liquor. Which was probably why the sneaky android insisted they meet and drink together at least once a month.

Risk always looked forward to those meetings. It was the only time they were all together, and even those events usually resulted in a few fights by the time the night ended. They were all brothers, but they were also all arrogant, stubborn, and solitary by nature. Well, everyone but him.

He was stubborn and maybe a little arrogant, but unlike his clanmates, he didn't enjoy solitude. He craved company. He moved his foot to brush it against Joy's bare leg. Now, he had Joy. She chatted to him about all sorts of things as he worked, filling the air with her words and soothing his soul with her presence.

"You've been working for hours. Can I get you anything? A drink of water? More pudding?" Her tone was light and teasing with a hint of desire that tempted him to abandon his task and pounce on her.

"I will have more *pudding* soon. For now, some water would be nice. Thank you."

Her attention and care warmed his heart and made him feel strange—not the rush of need that had driven him half out of his mind but something deeper. He didn't understand it, but he accepted it the same way he accepted the marks they both bore. They were meant to be together. She needed his protection, and he needed her in ways he hadn't dreamed of until now.

She left for a moment to refill his waterskin with the stale-tasting water from the shuttle's dispenser. He'd rather consume fresh water from the rivers and streams by his treehouse. He couldn't wait to show Joy her new home. Would she like the house he'd built for himself? If not, he'd change things until she was content. He'd have to find clothes for her, too. She could be naked when they were alone, but when his brothers were around? No. He'd cover her with every scrap of clothing he could convince Bysshe to fabricate for him and make sure she was never alone with any of them. They may be his brothers, but Joy belonged to *him*.

Joy's uneven footsteps marked her return. She still limped, though she managed to get around well enough inside the shuttle where the deck was flat and she could use the seats for balance.

She settled at his feet again and tapped his leg. "Hold out your hand and I'll pass you the water."

He did as she asked and was soon downing the contents, surprised at how thirsty he was. How had she known?

He had just set the waterskin down when he caught a whiff of something bitter. He breathed in deeply and recognized what it was. Pain medication.

"Is your ankle bothering you?" he asked.

After a moment's silence, she answered him. "It's not my ankle."

Was that fatigue he heard in her voice? Was she tired? It hadn't occurred to him that she might need more rest than he did. He began working his way out from beneath the console, but she placed a hand on his hip and pressed down hard enough to make him stop.

"I'm alright, Risk. I have a headache. That's all it is. There was an incident on the *Harvest* after the captain ordered me to get Maddison and Loris onto this shuttle and fly them to safety. The first officer didn't like that. She attacked me. That's when I hurt my ankle. I also lost consciousness when my head hit the deck. I think that blow messed up my sensors a little. I'm getting some feedback and distortion, but it's nothing I can fix right now. That's why I have a headache."

He growled in frustration. Why hadn't she told him she was in pain? Worse, he could do nothing to help her. The tech she used to see was far beyond his rudimentary training and abilities. The scrawnies had wanted them to be capable soldiers but not so capable they could find a way to escape.

Annoyed with himself, the situation, and his inability to find a way to defeat the lockdown, he thumped the underside of the console with a closed fist.

The circuitry rattled, a shower of dust fell on his face, and a wire he hadn't noticed before fell into view, dangling right above his face.

"Fuck!" he snarled and caught the wire in one hand while following it back to its starting point.

"What is it?" Joy asked.

"Whoever wired this console knew even less about this shit than I do. I think I found the problem."

She made a soft, excited noise that sent all the blood rushing to his cock instead of his brain, which was where he needed it right now. If this was what he thought it was...

He checked everything again and then a third time. Yes. Finally!

It only took a few seconds for him to attach the wire to its proper place. Now all they needed to do was power everything up. Before he did that, though, he scanned the cramped space one last time... and noticed another potential issue. A panel had come loose and hung askew. It shouldn't affect anything, but it was easier to fix it now than to have to crawl back in here later. He pushed it back into place, but something seemed to be blocking it from sealing properly.

He tried again, but now he was certain something was in the way. He tugged at the panel and it fell away easily. It hadn't been secured at all. His curiosity grew by the moment as he craned his neck to try and get a look inside the newly revealed space. It was too dark to see much, so he reached up and searched it by hand. He found a box stuffed inside the space. At least, it felt like a box. One wrapped in some kind of waterproof packaging. He removed it, set it down on his chest, and reached back inside to find yet another wrapped box. He pulled this one out, too. It was a different shape than the first one, but they were about the same weight. He managed to hold both boxes against his body with one hand and began pulling himself out from under the console with the other.

Joy got to her feet and shuffled backward to give him more room. His head was still inside the console when she lost patience and hit him with a steady stream of questions. "Did you fix it? Can we fly out of here in the morning? Oh, what have you got there? Those don't look like electronic components."

"Yes, I think I fixed it. No, I don't know what these are, but they are definitely not supposed to be stuffed inside the console. Whoever put them there must have knocked a wire out of place, and they didn't reconnect it properly. That's why you weren't able to reboot the system despite the captain giving Loris the codes."

At least, that's what he thought was wrong. No point in giving Joy any reason to doubt him. Either the shuttle would fly, or it wouldn't.

"And the boxes?" she picked her way carefully over

his out-stretched legs and leaned down to take one of the objects off his chest.

"Are boxes. That is all I know. Asking me questions I don't have answers to will only increase the time it takes to open these and find out what's inside."

Her cheeks darkened as she dropped her head. "Sorry."

"Sorry? No. You do not apologize to me for who you are. I have just never met someone so curious. Well, maybe Strife, but he is quiet about it."

She laughed and moved out of his way. "Didn't you say that Strife is mated to Clarissa. If he is the quiet, focused sort, I bet they're getting along quite well. Well, apart from her fear of open spaces." Joy went still. "Oh no. She was terrified every time we went planetside. She was born in space and never experienced open air like this. She can't be having an easy time of it."

"Strife will take care of her. You don't need to worry, little moon. He will protect her with his life. Just as I will protect you."

He intended his words to comfort her, but instead her expression soured for a brief moment. He had no idea why, so he decided to ask. "You don't want to be protected?"

A low sigh slipped from her lips before she raised her head and answered him, "I don't like anyone thinking I'm helpless. I know. I know. I'm blind. So sometimes I do need help, but that's not the same thing. I can take care of myself." Her mouth quirked into a ghost of a smile. "At least, that used to be true. Since I'm now trapped on a strange planet with no chance of being rescued but a good chance someone is going to try and kill me soon, I'm going to need more help than usual."

"And you will have it." He got to his feet and pulled her into his arms. "But only from me. If you ask one of my brothers for help, he might get stupid, and then I'll have to kill him. I like my brothers, so I'd rather not do that."

"You wouldn't," she said.

He kissed her hard before answering. "If they forget who you belong to? I would. All our lives we had to share what little we had. Even the pleasure bots the verexi provided. Now I have my own home, my own possessions..." he kissed her again, cupping the back of her head in his hand as he plundered her mouth. Once she was breathless and trembling in his arms, he stopped to say, "And now, I have you."

"I'm your little moon," she agreed and then smiled at him. "And you are my pudding."

He purred at her words, his body instantly aflame with the need to have her.

"You think I am tasty?"

"Definitely. Tastiest male in the galaxy. And I'm suddenly very hungry."

He glanced down at the boxes they both held. "And these?" he asked.

"Can wait until later. Though we should test the shuttle before we..." she trailed off.

"That can wait too. If it doesn't work, I'll need my brain working. Right now, I can't think of anything but what I want to do to you."

It was a reckless choice, but he didn't care. If having Joy now meant dying later, at least he'd die happy. After he killed as many of the enemy as he could, of course.

7

No one attacked them during the night, which made Risk glad he'd taken the time to pleasure his female. The sounds she made were the most beautiful things he'd ever heard, and her body fascinated him. She had soft, luscious curves he loved to explore, and her smooth skin had tiny constellations of something she called freckles. He liked those, too.

Once they were safely home, he would keep her in his bed for days, learning everything he could about her. He looked forward to that. So much so he was up before dawn despite their late night. The shuttle worked as it should now, and he intended to be airborne as soon as it was light enough to find his way to the ruins of the crashed ship that acted as the gathering place for their clan. Once they landed, he could update everyone there, and they could make plans to find Vengeance and Havoc as well as send word to the rest of the clan.

This would work. He could feel in his bones that this would be another good day. He had Joy, a functional ship, and two boxes of luxury contraband.

They'd gotten around to opening the two boxes eventually and discovered that one was packed to the brim with what Joy confirmed was some of the best chocolate in the galaxy. The other box contained genetic samples and seeds to grow more of the delicious stuff. He still couldn't believe something that good could be made from a plant. It just didn't seem right.

Joy had been equally excited and upset by the discovery. She was pleased they could have a supply of chocolate in the future. Her unhappiness came from the fact that the crewmember who attacked her had obviously been smuggling the stuff. That's why she wanted onto the shuttle—to get her contraband back. Joy estimated the two boxes were worth a fortune to the right buyers. He didn't care about their value to others. All that was important was that they valued it. Bysshe would figure out how to grow it, and the clan would enjoy it.

He left Joy asleep on the narrow bench she used as a bed. She was still naked, her coronet of sensors set carefully beside her so she could find it once she woke.

He'd slept on the floor beside her, listening to the sounds of her breathing and the rustle of blankets as she moved from time to time. She didn't stir as he opened the shuttle door and stepped into the still-dark morning.

The ship was their best protection, but it was confining and reminded him of his cell on the lunar base where they'd been held. After a lifetime of captivity, he loved the fresh air and open spaces of this planet. Living things rustled in the forest, some finishing their nocturnal hunts as others woke to face a new day. The breeze was heavy with moisture, an early warning of another storm coming this way. By the time it arrived, they'd be far away from this place.

The sky was already beginning to lighten with the approaching day, but he could still make out the silvery ring that encircled the planet. It would fade from view soon, but for the moment the shimmering line danced just above the horizon.

He would have liked to stargaze a little longer, but his bladder insisted he move on. The tiny space the humans used for such things was so small he couldn't use it, so he'd make do with the outdoors until he was home again. A new idea struck him as he made his way into the woods... sharing a shower with Joy.

Now that was an intriguing idea.

He was still thinking about sex with Joy in all kinds

of places around his house when he heard something...
wrong. A footfall that didn't sound like anything the
local wildlife would make. It was too heavy. Too
steady. Too... *fuck.*

Risk dropped to the ground and went completely
still, all thoughts of Joy shoved aside. He reached out
with his senses in an attempt to hear the sound again or
catch the scent of whatever was out here with him.

A clicking sound followed by two sharp pops
caught his attention, though the source of the noise was
too far away for his translator to parse what was said.
That had to be a liksik. But what was one doing out
here? The insectile race preferred trade to combat as a
rule and were generally peaceful unless provoked. But
no other species he knew of made those sounds.

A heavy footstep sounded from a different part of
the wood, and this time the wind carried the
distinctively unpleasant stench of a logaran. That
species lived for conquest and could be found in almost
every mercenary unit in the known galaxy. That was
all the confirmation Risk needed. They had to be
mercenaries sent to kill Joy and her friends so they
couldn't tell anyone the truth about what had
happened.

He growled softly and grinned to himself.

They thought they were the hunters, but they
weren't. They were his prey. He might have left the

firearm in the shuttle, but he had his personal weapons and his battle gear.

That's all he'd need to deal with these assholes. He wouldn't let any of them hurt Joy or take the shuttle away from him. They were his, and he would fight to the death to keep what he had rightfully claimed.

Faced with several options, Risk chose the one that kept Joy the safest. Instead of fighting the enemy here, he'd opted to lead them away from the shuttle. Since he couldn't see their ship, he had to guess at the number of mercenaries he faced. He'd already confirmed two, but at least one more would likely be out there. Three was a standard number for the scouts he'd come across before, so that's what he planned for. If there were more? Well, he'd just have to kill them faster.

It pained him to make deliberate mistakes as he moved, making just enough noise to bait the soldiers into following him. They couldn't have been here long or they would have shot him while he stared up at the sky. He hoped the others never learned about that. They'd mock him for months for being so careless.

Once he had them far enough away, he stopped making noise and circled back to put himself between them and the shuttle.

He found the liksik first. Its large, beetle-like carapace was not designed for traversing a wooded area with anything resembling stealth. Dawn had arrived, and color had returned to the world, which made the mercenary easy to spot. The vegetation on this planet tended to grow in shades of red, orange, and yellow. The gleaming black exoskeleton of the liksik was like a pocket of shadow trying to hide in a sunny meadow.

Thanks to his training, he knew the best ways to get past the mercenary's natural armor. It was a source of humor to all the fa'rel that the scrawnies had taught them how to take out the very same races they now sent to try to exterminate their failed experiments.

Risk crept up behind the liksik, using the soldier's blind spots to stay out of sight. He drew the largest knife he carried out of its sheath, grateful he hadn't been foolish enough to leave the shuttle without all of his weapons.

The approach took longer than the actual attack. He closed in as much as he dared and then rushed his target at full speed, his knife raised over his head and gripped tightly in both hands. He had to aim the strike perfectly, or it would slide off the armor and leave him facing an angry opponent with only one weak spot—an opening between the plates high on its back.

He hit his target, the blade sinking deep into the crack. The soldier uttered a stuttered burst of trills that faded even as it fell forward with Risk still hanging from his knife handle. He rode the corpse to the ground and waited two heartbeats to confirm it was dead. Then he rolled off and sprinted for cover before the other mercenary came to check on his newly deceased companion.

He didn't go far. Once he found a good hiding spot, he hunkered down and waited for the arrival of the second mercenary, the big logaran he'd scented earlier. It took longer than he expected for the second mercenary to show up. The lack of urgency made the hair on his neck and back stand up. Something wasn't right...

He dove to the ground a split second before a blaster pulse slammed into the tree he'd been crouched beside. The shot had come from somewhere to his left, but the logaran was in front of him.

Fuck. They were smarter than he expected and had tried to ambush him. He growled softly. Fine. If that's how it was, he'd go to his backup plan. *Kill them faster.*

He launched himself to his feet and raced toward his target, knife in one hand and his claws extended. Logarans were big, powerful, and dangerous, but they tended to be slow. He should have enough time to reach his opponent and get behind him so his bulk screened Risk from another blast.

He almost made it.

A searing pain tore through him as a plasma bolt slammed into his shoulder blade. He roared in pain but kept going, aware that if he stopped now, he was dead.

He acted as if he intended to charge into his quarry and then dodged to one side while the big creature was still raising his weapon.

He hit the ground hard and then scrambled back to his feet, lunging out with knife and claws to hamstring the enemy.

Green blood fountained from the wounds Risk opened on the back of the logaran's thick legs. Most of their armor was on their upper body, leaving them with exposed areas a faster, more agile opponent could take advantage of.

Risk had to dash away again as his enemy roared and collapsed to the ground, his crippled legs no longer capable of holding his weight.

It wasn't necessarily a fatal wound if someone arrived to do first aid and stop the bleeding, but that one was no longer a threat. That's all that mattered. Once he killed the third mercenary, he'd come back to finish off the wounded one.

The wound in his shoulder hurt like a bitch, and every breath he took came with a hint of burned fur and charred flesh. The logaran's blood wouldn't be doing anything good for the injury either, but he couldn't do anything about it right now. The scrawnies had modified their DNA to give all the fa'rel fast healing and a strong immune system. He'd recover and maybe have a new scar to remember this battle by. Joy could tend to his wound once this was over.

Joy. Thoughts of her made his stomach curdle with worry. He hoped she slept through this fight and only woke when it was over and she was safe. If anything happened to her...

He sprinted in the direction of the shuttle, driven by a sudden need to be certain she was not in danger. His feet flew, his one working arm pumping hard as he wove through the trees and leaped over bushes and fallen logs. His instincts screamed at him to move faster. He didn't understand the threat, but he ran faster anyway.

He didn't run fast enough.

A cry of pain and fear came from somewhere ahead of him, the sound of Joy's voice tearing holes in his heart. Someone would die for hurting his female, and then he'd kneel at her feet and ask forgiveness for failing to protect her the way he should have.

"I know you're out there, beast. And you know I have your pet."

Risk forced himself to stop and find a hiding place where he could see what was happening instead of charging out to meet the threat head on. If he died, Joy would be next. He had to be smart about this.

In the clearing by the fire pit stood another logaran. Judging by the pristine state of his gold and blue-trimmed armor, this was the leader of the crew, and he was an ugly son of a beast, even for a logaran. Bulbous features, a sneering mouth, and arms as thick as landing struts bulged from between the various pieces of his body armor.

The brute had one meaty, three-fingered hand wrapped around Joy's upper arm and held her up so high only the toes of her good foot touched the ground.

Her face was pale, her eyes wide with fear, and she had one of the blankets from her bed wrapped around her torso. She looked so small and delicate next to the bastard holding her.

Rage welled up and threatened to push him into a killing frenzy, but he fought for control and won. He wouldn't give in and do something stupid. His brothers had learned the hard way that it was better to be patient and make a plan. But what the fuck could he do that wouldn't get Joy hurt or killed? She needed him to protect her.. and he'd failed.

Then he noticed two things. Joy kept moving her hand, flicking her fingers in a subtle gesture that drew his attention to the knife sheathed on the logaran's hip.

The handle was close enough for Joy to reach it, but what could a blind woman do with a knife?

Then, he saw something else. Joy's coronet wasn't on her head but fastened around her neck somehow. Did that mean she could see? Instead of trying to make a plan, he took a moment to try and figure out what Joy's plan was.

Once he understood, his stomach twisted into a new set of knots even as his heart swelled with pride. His little moon was braver than he could have imagined.

He would not fail her again.

8

———

GETTING ATTACKED TWICE in a matter of days was not Joy's idea of a good time. Getting hauled out of her makeshift bed by a logaran with personal hygiene issues was now at the top of her "never do it again" list, and she was ready to be done with this day and go back to bed already. But first, she had to deal with the asshole who had just called her a fucking *pet*.

At least she'd managed to grab her coronet and fasten it around her neck. She didn't use that function much for a number of reasons. It wasn't comfortable, but more importantly, using it this way meant a slight delay between when it sent the data and when the image registered in her brain. The time lag was minute, but it still gave her a headache. Since the tech was already out of alignment, her headache had gone from annoying to excruciating.

She couldn't see Risk, but she knew he had to be out there. The big ass holding her wasn't talking that loudly, so he had to be certain Risk was close by. She fought back the pain and thought desperately. Her one advantage was that the logaran didn't know what the thing around her neck was. Damned fool thought it was a collar. That meant as long as she didn't look around, he'd assume she wasn't thinking of escaping. After all, he didn't know she was blind.

She'd spotted the huge knife in its sheath while they were still in the shuttle. It would be more like a sword in her hands, but she was confident she could wield it long enough to take this asshole down. Now, she just needed to let Risk know what she wanted to do. If she could at least weaken the one holding her, Risk could finish the job. From what she'd heard on the mercs' radios, only two of them were left, but they'd also mentioned that Risk was hurt.

That worried her. Was he alright, or was her mate bleeding to death somewhere out there?

Mate. The word resonated down to her soul. *Yes.* That was what he was. She'd finally found someone she wanted to spend her life with. There wasn't a chance in hell she was going to let anyone take him from her.

She gestured to the knife several times and hoped Risk understood what she was trying to communicate.

Hell, she hoped he was still alive and on his feet. She might be able to take one logaran down if luck was on her side, but no way could she handle two of them.

Something moved in the bush, and she caught a glimpse of golden fur and amber eyes looking her way.

He was out there, and by letting her see him, he was telling her he was ready to act.

With her heart in her throat and her blood roaring in her ears, Joy pretended to swoon, her legs almost buckling as she let all her weight hang off the logaran's meaty, three-fingered fist.

He snarled in annoyance and yanked her back up, which was exactly what she'd hoped for. She grabbed the handle of the knife as he manhandled her, his own movements masking what she was doing for several precious seconds.

She stabbed him in the side, right at the point two pieces of body armor joined together.

The logaran squealed like an angry animal, the sound surprisingly high-pitched for something so big. He tried to throw her off him, but she clung to the knife, working it back and forth with both hands as she dangled beneath his armpit, her feet not touching the ground.

The sheet she'd managed to wrap around herself fell off in the fracas, but she was too focused on what she had to do to worry about her nudity. If she survived, it would make the story that much more badass. If she didn't? No one would ever know the details.

Risk bellowed a war cry as he tore across the clearing. He was little more than a golden blur, and by the time she got the image, he was already leaping onto the logaran, snarling in fury.

She let go and dropped to the ground, her part of the fight over. That's when she remembered her sprained ankle. The joint gave way, and she fell to her knees, her arms outstretched to break her fall. Something in her wrist twanged in a very unpleasant way, and a spike of hot pain raced up her arm.

She yelped and cradled the newly injured limb against her chest. Dammit. Another injury. But at least this time she stayed conscious.

Not far away, Risk was tearing into the mercenary. He was violence in motion, and the bigger alien flailed at him with what looked like a blaster, but he was using it as a club, not a firearm.

The fight wasn't over when the second surviving mercenary stepped into view. He had his weapon trained on Risk, but it was obvious he couldn't take the shot without endangering his companion. She screamed a warning for Risk.

At that moment, he managed to take down the male he fought, blood gushing everywhere as the mercenary crashed to the ground hard enough she felt the impact. Risk crouched, grabbed something, and then spun around to hurl whatever it was at the approaching logaran.

It turned out to be the knife she'd stabbed her attacker with.

The blade bit into the armor beneath the mercenary's throat and sank deeply enough to do damage. The other male fell to the ground, clutching his neck and the weapon with both hands.

Joy covered her coronet to block the images, suddenly sickened by all the blood and death. She sat and waited as the horrible sounds of someone choking on their own blood abruptly ended. She didn't allow herself to see again until she heard Risk walk toward her.

"Are you alright, little moon?"

She wanted to sob and throw herself into his arms, but she just nodded and tried to smile instead. "I think I might have a broken wrist. That's all."

He crouched beside her, his fur matted with blood and his face twisted into an expression of concern and... regret? "I'm sorry. I failed you. You were hurt because I wasn't there to protect you."

Her laugh sounded brittle to her own ears, but it was better than crying. "What are you talking about? You did save me. They're dead. We're alive. That's all that matters, Risk. We're still here." She reached out to stroke his cheek. "You fought for me. You bled for me. If that's not love, I don't know what love is." Her laughter lightened. "And I'm a professional matchmaker. Love is my business."

"You *were* a matchmaker." He nuzzled her palm. "Now you are my little moon. And my little warrior. I will never think of you as helpless again."

"That's good. But honestly, I will be quite happy to leave all the fighting to you from now on. That was..."

"Killing is never easy," he agreed. "But sometimes, it's necessary."

"I know. That helps. Not much, but a little." She belatedly remembered that he'd been hurt. "How are you? I heard one of them report you'd been shot."

He winced. "It hurts, but I'll live. Will you nurse me back to health once we get home?"

He actually waggled his brows at her. "I need a lot of care and kisses. This is what I saw in the vids we were allowed to watch."

"I will give you all the care and kisses you want." Her smile warmed as relief replaced a little of her worry. "Right after you let me treat that injury."

He shook his head. "Bandage it to slow the bleeding. That's all. We need to leave before anyone else comes looking for their friends." He scowled.

"We'll have to leave their ship behind for now. There's no time to look for it."

"We'll come back, but you're right. We need to leave. And let the others know what happened."

"We do."

He got to his feet and offered her his hand. Standing up, she could see that one arm hung at his side, and he was clearly in pain. She was a bit of a mess, too. Between her ankle and her wrist, getting up wasn't easy. They both made their way slowly back to the shuttle, leaning on each other for mutual support.

Once inside, she fetched the first aid kit and did what she could to patch up his shoulder, using some expanding foamy stuff that sealed his wound and apparently applied a numbing agent to help with the pain. After that, he bandaged her wrist, and they laughed at the state they found themselves in. Battered, bruised and covered in blood from several species, neither of them was a pretty sight.

She cleaned herself up the best she could and then got Risk to help her into her pants. She sliced up one of the blankets and turned it onto a sort of tie-around top that covered enough of her to satisfy them both.

What will your brothers think when we show up looking like this?" she asked.

"They will think I have the bravest, most beautiful female of them all. And they will be right."

That answered earned him a kiss that turned into several kisses. Then they went to the cockpit. He needed her help reaching some of the buttons, and she was more than happy to assist. The sooner they figured out how to fly this shuttle, the sooner they'd be home.

It didn't matter that she'd never seen the place they were going. It was going to be her home for now... and maybe forever. The thought didn't bother her at all. In fact, it brought a smile to her lips. Home is where the heart is. That's what she'd told so many women when they had second thoughts about moving to another planet after they found their match.

Risk had her heart now. Wherever he was. That was home.

9

FLYING the shuttle was both easier and more difficult. Risk quickly adapted to the controls of this particular vessel and managed to apply what he knew well enough to operate the thing. However, his injured arm meant coordinating with Joy to get the job done, and that led to a few minor hiccups. And then came the landing...

They set down hard in a clearing near what had been their first home on this planet. The ship they'd arrived on had crashed, tearing through the forest and topping trees for the better part of a kilometer before slamming into the side of a large hill. The impact triggered an avalanche that partially buried the wreckage. The soil and debris provided extra protection against the elements during their first few months.

When he and his brothers had moved onto their own parcels of land, Bysshe had stayed at the original crash site. He kept their only functional fabricator running along with some elements of the ship's mainframe and power sources. The android also tended to an ever-expanding garden full of healing herbs to supplement their meager supplies and an orchard full of fruits he used to make the liquor they all enjoyed.

Despite his best efforts, the shuttle came closer to Bysshe's precious fruit trees than he intended, and by the time he and Joy had made their way to the doorway, the blue-skinned android had come out to meet them and to check on his crops. He was also armed and wearing some of the body armor they'd looted from the bodies of mercenaries who had come to kill them and failed.

"You didn't get my message that we were inbound?" Risk asked and gestured to his friend.

"I did, but messages can be faked." Bysshe shrugged. "I take it you reached the downed ship and retrieved this shuttle? How many survivors are there?"

Joy stepped into view beside him. "They didn't get to the *Bountiful Harvest*. Risk and his brothers found us on the way. Vengeance and Havoc are bringing my companions here by land. We got the shuttle running and flew... once we dealt with some mercenaries."

Bysshe's eyes narrowed as he scanned them both. "I see. Both of you show signs of shock and injury. I can send up a flare to bring the others. I've been informed Menace's mate has medical training, and Strife's female may be able to fly this shuttle." He looked at Risk. "You can get more training from her once you are healed up. Maybe then I won't have to worry about my orchard being flattened."

"Ha-ha. Funny," Risk retorted and then placed an arm around Joy. "This is Joy. She is mine."

"I gathered that. You share markings just like the others." Bysshe actually cracked a smile. "I am happy for you. Come down. I'll call for the others."

Then the android nodded at Joy. "I imagine you will wish to see the other females? They have been hoping more survived the crash."

"I would like that very much. Thank you, Bysshe."

"Of course. I've also got some fresh fruit that's safe for you to eat. I imagine you're tired of rations by now."

That made Joy laugh. "I am. But we did have some treats. Chocolate pudding. Oh! That reminds me! Risk said you are the gardener of this clan. We found something hidden on board and I think you should have it."

Risk growled softly. "The seeds he can have. The chocolate stays with us."

She patted his arm. "Of course it does, pudding.

We might have to share with the other women, though. We all love chocolate."

He chuffed and pretended to grumble, but if sharing their treat made Joy happy, he'd allow it. He'd allow a great deal if she kept calling him by that nickname. As ridiculous as it was, he liked it.

It took a fair number of growls, threats, and posturing to get everyone together in one room. Risk and his brothers glared at each other while watching their females cry and hug each other. The amount of emotion they showed made him uncomfortable, and his clanmates seemed to feel the same way. How could such small beings hold so many tears and feelings? It was baffling.

Eventually he and his brothers left the females to talk and went outside. He didn't like being away from Joy, but it was easier for him knowing that no other male could see her while he couldn't.

"Do you think the others are finding their mates, too?" Mayhem asked.

"I think Vengeance already has. He claimed the warrior female before we parted ways. She told him no, but if they experience the same thing I did? She will say yes soon enough."

They all laughed and nodded in agreement. It struck Risk that this was the first time they had all been together since the last group gathering, which felt like a long time ago. It was good to see his brothers again, even if all of them were growly and feeling protective of their new mates.

They shared their stories and tried to learn what they could about the human females from each other. All of them agreed they would need to speak to Bysshe about it soon. He was of human design and had to know the answers to their questions.

Strife's female came out to them sometime later. "Hope is looking after Joy's injuries right now. She'll be ready to treat you soon and asked you to come inside."

"I will do that. What will you and the others do now?"

Clarissa grinned. "I am going to fly that lovely shuttle you brought us over to the *Harvest* and see if we can't help with the rescue. The sooner everyone is away from that ship the better. Plus, that shuttle is armed. If the mercenaries arrive, we can use it to defend ourselves."

He liked that this female already considered them to be one group. It was not something any of them had ever imagined could happen. They'd assumed they would either die alone on this world or escape and live long enough to seek revenge against the scrawnies. Now, they had another choice.

"And when this is over, would you give me flying lessons? I have the knowledge, but today was the first time I actually flew."

"Your first time? Damn. I'm impressed. My first time I smacked into the side of a freighter and nearly breached my hull. Of course I'll help." She glanced at Strife. "If you promise not to growl and snarl the whole time."

"I do not promise anything of the sort." Strife folded his arms and glared at Risk. "But if you agree not to look at my mate too much, I will allow it. And I will know if you don't behave because I will be behind her. Watching you."

Clarissa laughed and leaned into Strife. "Stop it. We both know who I belong to."

Strife's entire body seemed to soften as he stared down at his mate. "We do."

Risk left them to talk and returned to check on Joy. Once they were both treated, he had plans for her, and they didn't include another shuttle ride.

It was time he took his little moon home.

10

Tired but happy. That's how Joy felt as she walked through the forest of this strange new world with Risk. Hope had managed to stabilize her ankle well enough she could walk without pain. Her wrist wasn't broken, only badly strained, and Hope had done all she could to speed up healing. Bysshe and Rissa had looked at her coronet and made some minor adjustments that eased her headache. They assured her they'd be able to fully repair and maintain it once they'd had time for a better look. They'd both managed to clean themselves up, too, which had been a welcome opportunity.

Risk's injury took longer to deal with, though he was now in better shape than she was. Their newly appointed medic had managed to regenerate most of the lost tissue and then instructed her lover to take it easy for a few days. "You'll be fine, but you'll heal faster if you don't try to lift heavy things or take on anymore mercenaries until I give you the all clear."

Seeing the others alive and well had gone a long way toward healing her heart, too. If Hope, Clarissa, and Bella had all made it, she had to believe at least some of the others had as well.

"How long do you think it will take Havoc and Vengeance to get here?" she asked.

"Tonight would be the earliest if everything went well. I suspect we won't see them until tomorrow morning, though."

"You don't think everything went well?"

"I think they will be too busy enjoying your friends' company to hurry home."

Her eyes widened. "All of them? You think Maddison and Havoc..."

"I hope all my brothers find happiness," was all he said. Then he gestured ahead of them. "My home is close. You'll see it soon."

Does it have windows? I hope so. I love looking at the forest. It's all so vibrant and beautiful. The moss is as thick as a carpet, too. I bet the rocks are almost comfy to sit on." The area where Risk and the others lived was deep in the heart of a lush forest that was more like a jungle. Red and gold moss covered everything with huge trees forming a massive canopy high overhead. Sunlight shone on the leaves, painting the air in shades of fire.

In the distance they could hear the sound of flowing water. Did Risk live by a river? She decided to ask him. "Is that water I hear?"

"A small river. Deep enough to swim in some spots and fast enough to let me use a few small hydroelectric generators to provide power."

"You have power? Out here?"

"Come see for yourself." He took her hand and led her past a stand of trees and into a clearing.

A few outbuildings sat out in the open, but she couldn't see anything she'd call a home.

"Look up." Risk pointed to a massive tree with a trunk so thick it seemed more like a building than a living thing. Then he moved his hand up.

"Oh!" Nestled in the branches of that large tree was a house. Walls, windows, doors, and even a deck that appeared to encircle the whole building. A staircase spiraled down the trunk, the steps level and solid with a rope railing on the outside to prevent accidents.

"That's a tree house," she said and then shook her head. "No. That's a tree mansion! How did you build that? Do you all live in homes like these?"

"We all helped each other to build our homes, and yes, they are all similar, though now we make changes help each one to be unique. We all have power, too, and running water of a sort. You will be comfortable here." He smiled at her. "Welcome home."

She hugged him tightly, careful not to jostle his arm. "It's gorgeous. And there's really a river we can swim in? I haven't gone swimming in so long. I hope I remember how." She took a quick breath and continued. "Can I see the house now? You might need to help me with the stairs because of my ankle. Do you think we need an elevator?"

He blinked at her. "Too many questions and much too fast. No, there is no elevator, but I can build one if you like. Yes, there is a river. And, yes, I want you to see everything, starting with the house. As for the stairs, I can help with that, too."

He crouched beside her and reached out with his good arm. She stepped in close and put her arms around his neck.

"Ready?" He wrapped an arm beneath her bottom and flexed once. "When I say go, you jump up."

"Ready."

"Go."

She hopped, he lifted, and in a few seconds he had her cradled in one arm while she clung to him.

"Now, we go home."

It had to be one of the most comfortable places she'd ever seen. It wasn't at all fancy, but everything was neat, well-made, and welcoming. Natural materials and recycled elements from the crashed ship melded together to create something unique, and despite the simplicity of it all, she couldn't see anything lacking. A food prep area included wood counters, a heating cube, and even a cooling unit.

A simple table had two stools, a bench covered in cushions had been taken from the ship, and the hard, wooden floor had been polished smooth enough she didn't fear splinters.

"It's perfect," she announced after she got a look around.

"It's not finished yet. I have plans to expand it soon. The others are already working on theirs. Soon they will come to help me. Then this place will be bigger and have more deck space. During the rainy seasons floods are common. It will be nice to have space to store things where they will stay dry."

"I can help with that. I mean, I don't know anything about building, but I worked in warehouses before I lost my sight. That's how it happened, actually. Workplace accident."

"You will not have any accidents when I'm around." He made it sound like a royal decree.

"We'll see." She pointed toward a set of open doors opposite the living area. "Is one of those the bedroom?"

"Yes it is."

He started shedding what little clothing he had, leaving it to fall on the floor as he hurried toward the doors. "I will give you a tour of the rest of the house later. Now, bed."

She followed, laughing as she tried to undress and walk at the same time. She gave up halfway there and stopped to strip off her shoes and pants.

Risk came back out while she was still undressing. He growled low and then walked over, lifted her up a few inches, and used his foot to pull away her pants.

"I said bed. Now."

"Who said you wear the pants in this relationship?" she demanded.

"Neither of us are wearing pants. What's your point?"

She laughed too hard to even try and answer.

They landed on the largest bed she'd ever seen in a tangle of limbs and laughter. He rolled them over until they were both on their sides, one of her legs draped over his as he kissed her hungrily, pouring fuel on a fire already raging out of control.

She caressed him everywhere she could reach, stroking over soft fur and hard muscle. She could have lost him today. That thought only intensified her feelings for him. Not just lust, but love, too.

She loved him. It made no sense, but it was true.

She loved him and they'd nearly had their story end before it made it past the first page.

"You were incredible today. I never doubted you'd come for me. I was worried, though. I hate that they used me to bait you." She huffed. "And called me your pet."

That made him laugh. "You are no one's pet." He moved back and looked at her with a fierce and loving smile. "He tried to use you, but you made him regret it. You were brave today. But remember this. I will always come for you. You are mine, little moon. No one will take you from me."

Pieces of her heart she thought long dead and broken fell back into place in an instant. With tears in her eyes, she kissed him again, thanking all the gods of all the stars that this wonderful male wanted her. He wanted her as she was, blind, graying, and full of flaws.

He cupped the back of her head in one big hand and slanted a hard kiss across her lips. She slid her hands into his hair and pulled him closer. After being so close to death, she needed to feel alive again.

With a groan he speared his tongue deep into her mouth and moved over her so she was pinned beneath him.

"Your shoulder!" she protested, but he ignored her.

"Pain is fleeting. Soon I will be feeling too much pleasure to notice."

He bowed his head, brushed a tender kiss to her brow, and then moved slowly lower, dusting a trail of delicate kisses from her cheek to her throat. He nipped her soft skin several times with his fangs and then kissed the sting away before moving lower.

She moaned, wanting more than he was giving her. Now was not the time for foreplay. She needed him. Inside her. Fucking her. Making all the bad memories of this day fade away.

"Please, Risk. Don't be gentle with me. Not this time. I need you wild. All of you. Now."

He raised his head, his amber eyes gleaming like molten gold now. "You want me wild?"

"Yes."

He broke into a loud purr as he moved up her body, shifting her legs apart to position himself between them. The thick length of his cock pressed against her entrance as he leaned down and kissed her again.

"Mine," he said, his voice as tender as she'd ever heard it.

Then he pressed her down into the soft furs and blankets that covered his bed and made his words come true—hip to hip, mouths locked together, his thick cock filling her impossibly full. Every movement sent ripples of pure pleasure throughout her body, and she knew it would only get better.

He kept his head bowed but pushed his body off of hers until he had space to move, and move he did. Long, slow thrusts had him withdrawing until she was nearly empty and then filling her again. On each downward thrust, the ridges of his cock slid over her clit, and soon she was moving with him, their bodies locked together in an erotic dance that made her head spin.

"Joy," he whispered her name between kisses as he rode her hard, his cock and tongue moving in synch as the rhythm of their lovemaking sped up, hurtling them toward climax.

"I love you," the words spilled from her without warning.

He stared at her and then grinned. "I think I love you too."

Then he was pounding into her again, his control shattering as if her words had undone him. His expression was one of rapture as they met each other stroke for stroke, and seeing his pleasure was all it took to send her over the edge. She orgasmed hard, her inner walls gripping his length so tightly she could feel his cock thicken seconds before he came.

Then they were locked together, lost in pleasure so deep she felt like she was drifting on a sea of utter bliss, each tremor like a wave that rocked her as she floated.

Later, when showered, fed, and resting

comfortably in each other's arms, she uttered a sigh of pure contentment.

"Do you think they've found the others by now?" she asked.

"I hope so. They'll need the weapons and armor Bysshe and the others will bring with them."

She snuggled in closer to him, seeking comfort. "And if the mercenaries get there first?"

"Then I imagine they will learn the same lesson I have." He kissed the top of her head.

"And what is that?"

"Human females are fierce warriors. They are not helpless or weak. I am sure your friends will find a way to fight the mercenaries." He chuffed softly. "And possibly my brothers too."

"Only if they act like Vengeance." She thought for a moment and then added, "Or Strife. Or Menace. Or Mayhem for that matter. Huh. I think maybe all your brothers are in for a surprise."

"I hope so, little moon. They deserve nothing less."

"I wish them good hunting. But for us, the hunt is over." She had everything she'd ever wanted, and so much more besides. Joy hoped the others found even a small fraction of what she had on this distant and dangerous planet. She'd found love, a home, and a male who tasted better than anything else in the world... even chocolate pudding.

***

Thank You for Reading Marked For Risk

Want to read Joy and Risk's special bonus epilogue? Sign up for my newsletter here: subscribepage.io/Bonuscontent

And if you would like to know how Havoc and Vengeance are doing on their escapades, stay tuned! In the mean time you're welcome to explore the rest of the Crashed And Claimed series.

Want to read more stories with book boyfriends
that are out of this world?

Check out Susan Hayes' other Science Fiction
Romance Series at
Susanhayes.ca

Crashed And Claimed

The Omega Collective
(Co-written with Mina Carter)

The Drift: Astek Station
The Drift: Nova Force

The Drift: Haven Colony
Star-Crossed Alien Mail Order Brides

ABOUT THE AUTHOR

Susan lives out on the Canadian west coast surrounded by open water, dear family, and good friends. She's jumped out of perfectly good airplanes on purpose and accidentally swum with sharks on the Great Barrier Reef.

If the world ends, she plans to survive as the spunky, comedic sidekick to the heroes of the new world, because she's too damned short and out of shape to make it on her own for long.

To contact her about her books or to arrange end of the world team-ups, you can email her at susan@susanhayes.ca.

For all titles by Susan Hayes, please visit her website:
susanhayes.ca